a different
me

a different me

DEBORAH BLUMENTHAL

ALBERT WHITMAN & COMPANY
CHICAGO, ILLINOIS

Library of Congress Cataloging-in-Publication Data

Blumenthal, Deborah.
A different me / by Deborah Blumenthal.
pages cm
Summary:"High schooler Allie, who has long wanted to get plastic
surgery, becomes online friends with two other girls who share her
obsession"—Provided by publisher.
[1. Identity—Fiction. 2. Beauty, Personal—Fiction. 3. Surgery,
Plastic—Fiction.] I. Title.
PZ7.B6267Di 2014
[Fic]—dc23
2014002089

Printed in the United States of America.
10 9 8 7 6 5 4 3 2 1 LB 18 17 16 15 14

Cover design by Jenna Stempel
Cover image © Nicole Hill Gerulat/Getty Images

For more information about Albert Whitman & Company,
visit our web site at www.albertwhitman.com.

To Ralph

PROLOGUE

I'm lying on a narrow steel table under a ghostly white light as big as a satellite dish. Four people in pale blue cotton gowns hover over me like medical angels with soft voices and cool, gentle hands—taking my blood pressure, covering me with a thick blanket, and swabbing my face with something that smells strong like medicine. Blue paper hats cover their hair and white masks hide their faces. All I can see are their eyes fixed on me.

I feel a hot pinch as someone slides a needle attached to a plastic tube into the inside of my outstretched arm. Almost instantaneously, everything grows heavier and I start to feel drowsy, sinking deeper and deeper into the quicksand of unconsciousness. Violins are playing in the background. At least I think I they are, but it's hard to hear because everything's getting floaty and fuzzy.

"How do you feel?" someone asks, as a hand gently squeezes my arm. I start to nod, because that's as much as I can do.

All I know for sure in those last few seconds of consciousness is that I'm going to wake up a different me.

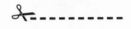

I'm always in the operating room in the dream, an icy white, impersonal, cavernous room in a big Manhattan hospital. Only each time I dream it, things around me are different. Sometimes the people and the voices change, or the look in their eyes. But it's always me under the hard, white light—outstretched, powerless, surrounded by strangers.

I'm anxious, unsure of what to expect. How long will it last? How will things turn out? Will something go wrong? Will I be asleep? Will I feel anything? Will it hurt? Will I bleed? Will I die?

I'm always scared. Always.

But I'm never sorry I'm there.

ONE

We have lobsters at the Palm to celebrate.

It's a fancy restaurant that doesn't look fancy. No giant vases with Polynesian flowers. No tropical fish tanks or cascading waterfalls. What it does have are steaks as big as saddles, brontosaurus-sized lobsters, and checks to match.

We don't come here a lot, but trumpet roll, it's my fifteenth birthday and my parents make a huge deal of it. I do a decent job of feigning surprise when the waiter in the pressed, tan jacket with his name stitched over his heart—Adam—appears at the table after they clear our plates. He holds out a wedge of devil's food cake on steroids. There's a flickering candle on top.

Suddenly our table is surrounded by jubilant waiters with barrel chests and voices as strong as opera singers. At the top of their lungs, they sing "Happy Birthday." I think they've added a few stanzas because it seems to go on and on and on.

Conversation stops at the other tables, and everyone in the room stares at me because clearly I'm the first person in the world to have a birthday.

The center of attention is not a place I like to be.

I slump down in my seat ever so slightly, not that it helps. I'm drowning in the limelight. My hands reach up and form a tent around my mouth and nose. My face gets hot, which has nothing to do with the burning candle that's lighting my face from below like a beacon so that I must look like...Never mind.

"Make a wish," my mom says.

"What you really want," my dad says.

He's obviously thinking a goal in life, not a Tiffany ring or Tory Burch flats.

Easy.

I look across the table at Jen, my closest friend in school. Even she doesn't know.

I stare at the lone pink candle as if the sparkling flame holds some higher universal power, some cosmic force that can propel me wherever I want to go if I summon it. I close my eyes and hear the words inside my head.

This year, I want the surgery. This year, I want to turn into a different me.

Whoosh! I blow out the candle hard to make it happen.

"Don't tell," my mom says.

As if I would.

TWO

It's two in the morning. It's not my birthday anymore, but we're still up talking about everything in the world. I've closed the blinds so my bedroom is dark. Jen is on the futon, but neither of us is sleeping. It feels like we're alone on a private island. I light a small candle that heats drops of lavender oil, infusing the room with a sweet, calming perfume. It's cozy to talk in the safe, interior world of the dark.

"So, Allie, what did you wish for?" Jen says.

Can't jinx my wish. I reach for the obvious. "For Josh Ryan to dump Amber and fall totally in love with me."

"That's definitely what I'd wish for," Jen says. "When he passes me in the hall, I get short of breath." She snorts. "I don't even get the feeling that Amber likes him, you know? The world's biggest stud follows her around like a dog and she hardly looks at him. Can you imagine?"

"I can't imagine, but it's not like I haven't tried."

I lie back on my pillow and stare at the ceiling where I've glued a sky full of white plastic stars that glow an eerie yellow-green in the dark.

"I wonder how it would feel to be Amber Augusta Bennington. You think she wakes up every morning and looks into the mirror and knows she's one of the best-looking people on the planet?"

"Of course she does," Jen says. "I mean what could she possibly find not to like?"

She socks her pillow and slides down under the blanket. "You'd think being gorgeous would at least make her nice. But I swear she never talks to anyone. She never even smiles." Jen makes a sound like she's trying to force something horrible out of her throat.

"If other girls are catty, Amber Augusta Bennington is a mountain lion of bitchiness and attitude."

"Amen," Jen says.

"That is not to say I wouldn't trade my body for hers. Or turn down her translucent ivory skin or her long, platinum hair." I stop there, blow out the candle, and slide under the covers too.

What I don't say as my eyes start to close and I drift into sleep is that more than anything else in the world, I'd take Amber Augusta Bennington's small, slender, perfectly sculpted nose.

Just that. That would be all. Then everything in my life would be different. And better. I'd be popular and get invited everywhere by guys who look like Josh. People would never laugh about me behind my back, or in front of it, and I'd scale the walls of my prison of unhappiness and be free of it, once and for all.

THREE

After Jen leaves at eleven in the morning, my mom surveys the damage. She shakes her head as though she can't believe the nightmare in front of her.

"You have to clean up this room." She starts collecting magazines, clothes, and candy wrappers and holding them out to me like a prosecutor presenting evidence in a courtroom.

"It's clean."

"This is clean? I'm sorry, but if it's not cleaned up by the end of the day, you're grounded." Her parting gesture is to try to slam a jammed dresser drawer closed. "What's behind here, a dead cat?"

She struts out and closes the door behind her. "Being grounded is not going to happen," I say, even though I know she can't hear me.

I start by hanging up stuff and throwing out old school

papers. I wedge my hand behind the drawer and yank out a mashed push-up bra. I continue pulling out clothes that have fallen overboard, and under a wadded-up T-shirt, I find Mr. Potato Head.

My blast-from-the-past favorite toy.

I got him when I was five and I still love him. I used to play with the eyes, the stick-out ears, the broad nose, the too-small top hat, the spindly little arms, the big red mouth, and even his tiny, brown pipe, putting one part in the hole where another belonged. I'd laugh at how he looked with his eyes poking out of the ear holes and his nose stuck on top of his head like a hat.

When it comes to real people, though, there's little room for changing the way the features sit on the face. On mine, specifically, the nose doesn't get the same grade as my green eyes or my clear skin. It's too big and the bump needs to be chiseled off.

The weird thing is, I didn't realize that until I looked at a video of Field Day taken at summer camp when I was almost twelve. Everyone was laughing about how they looked in the three-legged race, but what I fixated on was how freakishly big my nose looked, especially with my hair pulled back in a ponytail.

At one point the camera was almost in our faces and we were laughing hard, and then I turned so that I was in full profile. My nose seemed to fill the whole screen. It was gross. I looked at myself and felt sick. The camera abruptly moved on to another group of campers, and then it was in their faces, but I looked away. I didn't want to watch anymore. All I could think about was how I looked. Up until that moment, I never saw myself. I mean, I never truly knew what I looked like.

I was going to tell my mom, but I didn't. As crazy as it sounds, I looked at her differently after that because she has a bump too, only hers seems to go with her face more than mine does. Anyway, she's my mom and older. Looks don't matter as much to her.

But the hardest thing is when you realize that other people notice too. That it's not just you. You become a perfect target.

I was in a coffee shop with Jen and Katie a while ago. Two guys came in and sat opposite us. They were doing mature things like sticking french fries up their noses and snorting. Then they started looking over at us and laughing.

"Nose job," one of them said, staring right at me. His friend laughed and then punched him. "Shut up," he said.

But it was too late.

I pretended it was nothing, but my face couldn't hide it. "You wear your heart on your sleeve," my mom once told me. I wanted to cry, but I couldn't say anything or get up and run out, so I sat there, powerless to change the wounded look that I knew was on my face.

Jen looked at me and then back at them. "Assholes," she said. Katie pretended to barf.

I left my half-eaten hamburger and we asked for the check.

Another time I was in Bloomingdale's looking at makeup, because I'm obsessed with it, always looking for new products to try. I was walking down the aisle when a makeup artist held out a bottle of a new foundation.

"You have beautiful skin," he said. "Would you like to try some? We're having a special offer with a free makeup kit today."

I hesitated, and that was enough encouragement for him. "Sit down, please," he said. "It will only take a moment."

The backless stool was near the aisle so everybody walking by could see me, like I was on display. He dotted the foundation on my forehead and cheeks and kept telling me how it made my skin look even smoother. He kept saying, "Beautiful skin, beautiful." The corners of my mouth turned up into a smile. I unclenched my fists. Confession: I didn't get compliments, and even if he was a salesman for the company, he acted like he meant it.

Only a moment later he said he'd put a darker shade down the sides of my nose and a lighter stripe down the center to "camouflage it just a bit." That was it. He was trying to hide my nose and make it look smaller, but makeup couldn't do that. His comment threw me, and I started to sweat.

I wanted to get up and run, only I couldn't because he was staring down at me, working so intently on trying to fix me, to make me look better—but it was useless. I got so hot in my heavy coat that I thought I would faint. I never told anyone what happened because I couldn't deal, but I kept replaying it in my mind, and it made me squirm.

A few days after my fourteenth birthday, I planted the idea for the surgery. I remember the time because my birthday cards were still hanging over the slats of the doors between the kitchen and the dining room.

By then I had read stories online and in magazines about girls who had their noses done and how it totally changed the way they looked and felt about themselves. It didn't seem like a big deal at all. They went to a doctor's office in the morning, and by the afternoon, they were home in their own beds again. They weren't movie stars or models, the ones I read about. They were average girls like me.

One, two, three. I took a deep breath, then I tiptoed up behind my mom.

"When I'm a little older, I want to have my nose done."

There it was. Out.

I held my breath and waited.

She was emptying the dishwasher, about to put a blue-flowered dinner plate up on the shelf in the cabinet. Instead she reached back and turned to face me, holding the plate in front of her like a shield. A curious look crossed her face, as if she was trying to get a fix on what I was saying.

"Why?"

"Duh, because I hate my nose."

"That's a big decision. It's surgery."

"I realize it's a big decision and 'it's surgery.'"

"Well, you're too young now anyway," she said, obviously relieved the issue could be put off.

How did she know?

The sound of clattering dishes ended the discussion. She was caught short and couldn't deal. I could have insisted or brought my dad into the conversation, but what would have been the point? Fifteen or sixteen was the earliest age most doctors would do it anyway.

At least she knew now. The seed was planted.

FOUR

I head out of the library after school on Monday and walk toward the front door, going down a long corridor past a wall of grass-green lockers with dangling combination locks. At the end of the row I spot Amber's locker. You can't miss it—it's the one with a picture of her on it. A giant picture. I remember the day she put it up. Jen and I were walking out of the cafeteria when suddenly she froze.

"Look," she said, grabbing my arm. "One of Amber's modeling shots is covering her entire locker door like wallpaper."

It was gridlock in the corridor with everyone looking. Josh practically humped her locker door.

"You'd think it was the *Mona Lisa*," Jen said.

"That may have been the look she was going for."

"Look at her eyes," Jen said. "Staring into the distance as though she's pondering some galactic mystery."

As I study Amber's picture I'm struck by the confidence level it takes to do something like that because I could never in a million years cover an entire locker door with a giant blow-up of myself. That basically explains everything about confidence and how it lets you show yourself off to the world without the least bit of hesitation or concern about how it might come back to you.

It's clear to me now that the world is made up of only two kinds of people: those who are totally okay with posting pictures of themselves the size of the Great Wall of China and B-listers like me who are self-effacing because their faces turned out far from ideal, due to some inexplicable roll of the genetic dice.

✂ - - - - - - - - - -

Fortunately, I have control over some things in my world—like school. So I work hard, and except for math, my grades are decent, especially in English. But a handful of kids in our class don't get A's or even B's, sending the class average south, even though Mrs. Meyers never takes the low road by giving surprise quizzes or slipping words we haven't gone over onto tests.

This morning, the towering Mrs. M.—nearly six feet tall, wide as a battleship, and shrouded in a shapeless dress with sturdy oxford shoes from World War I or something—stands in front of the room looking out before removing her tomato-red bifocals.

This is a sign that she has something major to tell us—and it's not that we're moving on to a new act in *Julius Caesar*. I imagine it will be a pep talk about how the class has to snap to and get our grades up. Since it's only the middle of the semester, there is still enough time, praise the Lord.

My mom heard at the last Parents' Association meeting that they were talking about giving the teachers with the highest-scoring classes a year-end bonus, so I'm expecting a rally-the-troops speech.

But it doesn't turn out that way. Mrs. M. has a plan.

"The stronger students will mentor those who need help," she says, clasping her hands together, proud of her innovative idea. "And the effort will benefit both members of each team."

Translation:

1. I will be doing Mrs. M.'s job.

2. I will be stuck trying to help a perpetual zoner, in addition to doing my own work.

"We'll divide the class into mentors and students," Mrs. M. says, her enthusiasm already starting to grate on me. That's the signal for me to eyeball the room, guessing who I might get paired with and how this may play out. Just a few of the possibilities:

1. Josh Ryan. Tall, dirty-blond, intensely hot and definitely ready for his close-up. (Think half-naked greeter model at the door of Abercrombie, his summer job.) But Josh's chiseled body doesn't make up for the fact that he's not

only terrible in English, but also terribly unavailable because he's going out with Amber. He might as well have his forehead tattooed "Private property."

2. David Craig. A dick who carries a camera 24/7, dresses like a goth, and wears black eyeliner because he has this thing about Billie Joe Armstrong. He fancies himself a photographer because he once won an amateur snapshot contest. Now he thinks it's cool to stick his camera in someone's face while they're blowing their nose or dying from an asthma attack. Perpetual picture-taking obviously takes priority over studying English.

3. Harry Thomas, aka the sicko. Not only is he bad in English, but he's also a gag-worthy human being who picks his nose and has a bizarre fascination with insects. Excels at bio, especially when they murder and autopsy frogs.

4. Janelle Haney, a transfer student from a school somewhere in the Midwest that was horrible. Even though she works hard, she's behind by at least a grade.

5. Kirk Morrison. A star football player who's academically challenged and views school as an annoyance that gets in the way of kickoffs. Every girl in the school would like to dropkick him because of the slimy way he treats them.

I'm so busy casing the room that I don't hear Mrs. M.

"Alexandra," she says impatiently, even though everyone else calls me Allie. Before she utters another word, I know exactly who I'm not getting because I see her piercing eyes zero in on the last row, and that is not where Josh Ryan is sitting. "You work with Amber."

Amber?

I look at Mrs. M. and shrug. "Sure." I turn to look at Amber, who squeezes her eyes shut and shakes her head slightly.

FIVE

I'm edgy and uncomfortable about meeting Amber in the school library at five o'clock and spending an entire hour going over vocab words with her.

It's only sixty pathetic minutes of mentoring, but I'm still intimidated. I'm good in English, so I shouldn't be, but this isn't about English. It's about me. It's about worthiness. How pathetic is that?

"I totally dread the thought of mentoring Amber," I tell Jen.

"She's the one who should be embarrassed."

"It's not..."

"I get it," she says. "How long have I known you?"

To buck myself up, I try to convince myself that at some level, Amber is probably just as nervous about working with me. She might feel completely dumb because she repeatedly fails the vocab tests and can't even fill in the blanks to show she knows the tenses. Maybe needing extra help bothers her and she dreads coming face to face with someone in her class who knows she's never pulled more than a C.

Those thoughts flit around in my head as I sit and wait.

And wait.

Because even though we're supposed to meet at five, it is now ten after on my Swatch watch, eleven after on my phone, eight after on the library clock, and Amber is nowhere to be seen.

Just as I'm making an annoyed face, *click.* I look up. David Craig has taken my picture.

"What the hell?" But by then he's gone, probably off trying to catch somebody *else* looking pissed off or whatever his pictures are trying to show.

I text Jen. (Can you believe Amber? She's still not here.) I start my homework, lecturing myself on being too anal.

Maybe:

1. She had to go home after school and got stuck waiting for the bus to take her back.

2. She went home sick. She didn't have my cell, so how could she reach me?

3. She was run down by a cab and went to the ER where a

trauma team tried to jump-start her heart. How could she possibly get word to me?

I hang out a little longer, just in case.

Five fifteen, five twenty. At five twenty-five, Jen answers: Tell me you're not still there.

Home, I reply, embarrassed.

I swing my backpack off the floor and over my shoulder. Pointless to hang any longer. If Amber shows now, I'll look like a complete loser for just sitting there waiting, as if I don't have a life. I head out of the library and walk toward the front doors, passing the lockers. I spot Amber's locker again. A nanosecond pause and I move on.

The last thing I want or need is to be caught gazing at it, mesmerized, like some lame groupie. I make my way out to the street where a dozen kids are milling around, half of them on their cells. A few cars are double-parked out front, some with parents behind the wheels waiting for their kids, and others with kids in the driver seats, windows down, so people will assume they drive all the time even though they probably got their permits yesterday.

As I walk past a black Lexus that looks empty, I hear the low sound of laughter through a half-open tinted window. First a girl. Then a guy. I can't help but turn to see who it is. That's when I notice strands of blond hair fanned out on the black leather backseat and a blond guy whose face is pressed against the girl's. I pause for just a millisecond as the guy moves his head to the side, and I get a clear view of her small and perfect nose.

✂- - - - - - - - - -

"Did you at least tell Meyers?" Jen says the next day at lunch as she scrapes every drop of yogurt from the container with a vengeance. True to the stereotype about redheads, she has a short fuse. When something hits her wrong, alarm bells go off. But after being stood up, I can do without an interrogation by the truth police.

I glance at her briefly, then look away.

"Well?"

"No."

"Why not? She doesn't show up. She doesn't call. She's such a complete bitch." No one could ever accuse Jen of giving someone the benefit of the doubt.

"I don't know," I say. I honestly don't.

"So what did you both tell Meyers when she asked how the hour went?"

"Amber said she looked for me in the library but couldn't find me. She said she hung around and then left."

"And you let her get away with that?"

My right eyelid starts to twitch. I rub it so I don't look like a complete freak. "I told Meyers something came up and I had to reschedule."

Jen fixes the drama-queen stare on me, hands crossed over her chest.

"Am I missing something?" she says, crumpling her lunch bag into a ball and pitching it into the garbage.

"Allie," she mutters before she turns to go, "get a life."

SIX

I have a life, only sometimes it doesn't feel like I'm the right size for my own skin. Am I the only one not secure in the role of being myself? It's not something you can just bring up, like asking what you're wearing to the party on Saturday. I could just imagine asking Jen.

"Uh, nooo," she'd say, like I'd completely lost it. Why should she feel that way? She's not crazed about how she looks.

So I don't sit on my bed and take magazines quizzes like the ones that ask: "Do You Make the Grade? Find Out How Much You Love Yourself." I know how they would come out.

You're not happy with the way you are...

You're overly concerned with how other people see you...

What's worse is that I'm haunted by stupid remarks that people make. "Hey nose," Kirk called out to me one day on the way to the cafeteria.

And that was kind—for him.

My mom opened the door the last time I took one of those quizzes and I slammed the magazine down.

Sometimes I think my mom should have stayed with acting because her dramatic expressions tell you exactly what she's thinking. Her blue eyes narrowed slightly so that I could see creases between her eyebrows. She pushed her dark, shoulder length hair away from her face and studied me.

"It's a stupid self-assessment quiz, okay?" I held it out to her briefly.

Her face relaxed. "I wouldn't read too much into a psychological test in a teen magazine." She sat on the edge of the bed and I stared at the antique gold locket around her neck. My dad bought it for her on their tenth anniversary.

"Then again if you're unhappy, maybe it would help to talk to someone."

"Someone?"

"A shrink." She shrugged. "Just an idea."

Or a surgeon.

You can't just start talking to my parents about important things. You have to pave the way slowly because everything they do takes forever.

New job for my dad: two years and a bajillion phone calls, emails, letters, and lunches later.

Search for new couch: one year and about eighty gallons of gas to visit every furniture showroom.

New laptop for me: three months, but only because there was a sale.

"I'll think about it."

She nodded and stood, picking up a single shoe from the floor and hanging it on the shoe rack in my closet. She closed the door behind her on her way out.

The truth is that the way I see myself would change completely if I had my nose done. Then if I was taking a quiz about myself, everything would be yes, instead of no.

"Do you see yourself as beautiful?"

Or, more importantly, "do you see yourself as worthy of someone's love?"

It's nothing a shrink could fix. They're always asking how you feel, at least according to Jen and a show I watched on TV about a therapist and his patients. They expect you to talk and think about everything, even if you don't want to, and all they do is sit there and wait and make you feel dumb and self-conscious. My problem is obvious. A nose. It's there. You can't deny it, so what is there to discuss?

Jen went to a shrink after her favorite aunt died unexpectedly, and she ended up unhappier.

"You spend almost an hour unloading and then they give you this blank stare and say, 'So how do you really feel?'" she said. "Or worse, 'I'm sorry, our time is up. Let's continue next time.' That makes you doubly depressed because the last thing you want when you're talking about your loser life is to stop in the middle and wait a whole week to start talking about it again."

Surgery is faster. Therapy with a knife.

I hit Google and typed the ugliest word in the English language into the search box: rhinoplasty.

Translation: nose job.

Somewhere in the middle of the listings I came upon a website called The Swan. It includes bulletin boards about beauty and plastic surgery. People leave comments, but they also post pre- and post-op pictures and ask for feedback. They bitch about procedures and doctors, ask for recommendations of surgeons in their area, or just vent about things they need to get off their chests.

Click. I'm anonymous. I decided to call myself A.

So I began.

A: I'm desperate to get my nose done. No one I know needs the surgery so I feel dumb talking to anyone else about it. If anyone had any idea what I was obsessed with 24/7, they'd think I was a freak, you know?

When I checked back, I saw that a girl had welcomed me to the site, telling me "not to feel like a freak."

"Everyone thinks they're the only one who obsesses about their nose or whatever else," she said. "So welcome to the club."

Other posts were responding to someone trying to decide which of the three LA doctors she'd seen to go with. Someone else talked about how her nose was so swollen she couldn't tell how much the surgery helped. As I was about to close the screen, someone named Melanie answered me.

Melanie: A, I'm consumed with my nose too. Every time I look in the mirror—and I look in every mirror, even my reflection in store windows!—I'm reminded how much I hate the way I look.

I went to get a snack, and when I came back, there was a comment from another girl.

Katrina: Mel and A, I know how you both feel. I'm obsessed, 24/7.

Melanie: No one except my mom and my boyfriend know how much I hate my nose.

Katrina: I haven't told anyone at all.

A: It's just not the kind of thing you feel safe bringing up because if someone didn't think about it before, they'll never *not* think of it after you talk about it.

Melanie: My mom took me to a plastic surgeon when I was ten, but he told me it was too early to do it.

For the next few days, I went back to the site every night after dinner. It started to feel like a private universe where I could finally open up. Mel was always there. Katrina less so, but once the three of us connected, we had a routine—eight o'clock weekday nights, except for Tuesdays when Katrina does volunteer work.

Katrina: Have any of you seen a surgeon recently?

A: No, and my parents have no idea how much I think about doing my nose. More than anything, I wish I could go to one of those free consultations because then, at least, I'd find out what could be done.

Melanie: I'm sure whatever you look like, they can help you. Do you spend hours looking at all the before-and-after pictures on the plastic surgery websites like I do? Can you believe the difference an hour of surgery can make? What did people do before surgery? And before the Net? LOL! Who did they talk to about all this stuff?

Katrina: Can't imagine. Maybe all their secrets went into their diaries.

A: LOL! I'd be afraid someone would find mine. How old are you guys?

Melanie: 16.

A: 15.

Katrina: I'm 15 too.

For the first time in my life I was spilling all my feelings to faceless people in the virtual universe who got me better than anyone I know in real life. How weird is that? Out of the blue, I was flooded with relief. It was all out there, not locked in my head anymore. There were other people who felt the same way I did. I wasn't a total freak.

Now, after only a few weeks, our lives feel bound together.

One thing we all agree on: "You can't escape the mirrors."

Sometimes I laugh because a lot of what we talk about sounds like it's off someone's blog.

Melanie: Did you ever notice how different lights in dressing rooms—neon (deadly) or incandescent— can totally change the way you see yourself?

Katrina: I hate to go to the hair salon because a light just above the chair spotlights my nose. It makes me look totally gross.

Katrina is from a woodsy New Jersey town I never heard of where there are supposed to be black bears. Mel, as she calls herself, lives in Westport, Connecticut, near the water. Unlike my parents, Mel's sound totally cool.

Melanie: They think if I can fix my nose and look a hundred times better, why not? Plastic surgery isn't a big deal for them. You have a problem, you take care of it.

But that doesn't settle it for her. She has to deal with Mark, "the boyfriend."

Melanie: I've been going out with him for almost a year, and he doesn't want me to do it.

A: Why not?

Melanie: His older brother had surgery for a burst appendix and nearly died, so now he can't imagine why anyone would go near a hospital if they didn't have to. Not only that, but he likes the way I look.

Doesn't care about the bump—he doesn't want me to look like everybody else.

A: What are you going to do?

Melanie: Do *not* know.

Katrina doesn't have a bump, "just a crooked nose." She says she has a black belt in tae kwon do, a super-fit body, and long, blond "boy magnet" hair, as Mel calls it.

Katrina: Still, whenever I look in the mirror, I hate what I see.

Mel: Hate, that's the operative word here.

A: Amen.

SEVEN

The next morning, I morph back to the real world. I'm supposed to meet Amber for mentoring at five. In English I slip her a scrap of paper with my home address so I won't be stuck waiting in the library if she doesn't show. Only this time, I'm not going to roll over and play dead if she stands me up. It's called pride.

"If she pulls something today, Mrs. M. will hear about it so she gets a big fat F and I get another partner," I tell Jen as we leave school together.

"I wouldn't put it past her," she says.

When I get home, I drop my backpack on my bed and go to the fridge. I take out the milk and pour it over Special K with strawberries. Like magic, the milk changes the look of the berries, bringing them to life.

I carry the bowl to my room and check my phone for texts. There's one from Jen.

Barf-bag David C took a picture of me today a second after I slipped on the staircase. What is it with him?

I don't tell her about him taking a picture of me in the library because she already thought I was a douche for waiting so long for Amber. I text back: I'm glad I didn't get him to mentor—can you imagine?

On Facebook, Melanie links me to a sale at Nordstrom. I go online to look at cool leopard sneakers and a matching messenger bag, ignoring the baseball cap because it would flatten my hair and red flag my nose. I delete the usual garbage from my email account and start my homework.

The red digital numbers on the clock radio flash 4:45. What are the chances that Amber will show?

I go to the mirror and study myself. It's raining outside, and humidity does not work in my favor. I brush my hair hard, then harder, finally hurling the brush across the room. My ceramic straightener. Where the hell is it? I know I left it in the bathroom, but it isn't there. I discover it half hidden under my bed. Section by section, I straighten my hair.

After all the times I've straightened it, you'd think it would know by now and just give up. I look at the clock.

Four forty-six.

Four forty-seven.

Four forty-eight.

Will she at least call if she doesn't come, or is she just a total screwup?

At four fifty-five, the intercom buzzes.

"Amber is here," the doorman announces.

I shouldn't be surprised, but I am. Why did she show this time? Was Josh Ryan out with his mentor?

Instead of ringing, she knocks softly. She's wearing a fitted, black down jacket over black jeans and black high tops, and has a black backpack over her shoulder.

"Hi," she says, smiling.

Oddly enough, I think about whether she might be concerned with making a good impression.

"C'mon in."

She follows me to my room. Does she feel guilty about not showing for our first meeting and then making up a story to get out of trouble? She unzips her jacket, tosses it on the bed, and flops down on the floor.

I glance over at her, trying to ignore the sinking sensation that settles over me whenever I'm around Amber—this aching gut feeling that I'm inferior, an unappealing face in the crowd who fades to black around this standout, über-cool celebrity. I know that's ridiculous and sick but I can't help it, so maybe I do need a shrink. I sneak in a deep breath and turn to her.

"You want to start with the vocab words?"

"Whatever."

"Did you look them over?"

She raises an eyebrow like, are you serious?

"Well, look at them now. I'll get us some juice."

In the kitchen I search for two matching glasses and fill them with OJ. Would she rather have soda? But I'd look completely dumb to go back and ask her now after I said I was getting juice.

To give her time, I stare out the kitchen window and watch a woman trying to walk a golden retriever who's zigzagging her left and right like they're on a slalom run, a perfect routine for America's funniest pet videos. I can't decide who I have more sympathy for—the owner tugged in all directions, or the dog who's pulling her. Next I play with the magnetic letters on the fridge, rearranging them in an arc to spell my name.

I yank open the door and case the insides, peeling back the aluminum foil covering different-sized bowls and plates, hoping for a clue of what's for supper. Salmon from the night before. Pasta with pesto from before that. The usual vanilla and strawberry yogurt, fruit, and some nasty cheese with blue veins from France that looks like it dates back to Louis XIV. We never have anything decent. I slam the door and go back to the bedroom.

She's staring at the cards. Even if she learns the words, will Amber Augusta Bennington or anyone else actually sprinkle their sentences with "discordant," "lachrymose," "internecine," or "festoon"? What century is this?

She sips the juice and I wait until she's finished studying the cards. For the first time I notice that she's wearing two narrow silver bands on her ring finger. Each one has a small, shiny stone on top in a blue-green color.

I don't make any attempt at small talk because I can't think of anything to talk to her about. We don't have the same friends. She has a boyfriend. I don't. Her clothes are way nicer than mine, and even if I had her wardrobe, none of it would look as good on me. Aside from her face, there's a world of difference between being five foot six, average, okay body, and—drum roll—statuesque five-ten, single-digit size, and whippet thin runway body. So what is there to say?

Have you done it with Josh?

Is he good?

Any tips on popularity to share?

Any suggestions for making me look like a clone of you?

I wonder for the millionth time whether she wakes up every morning and looks into the mirror with a wicked grin on her face because she's way better looking than 99.9 percent of the girls in the world.

Or is there something about the way she looks that she doesn't like? If Amber fixates on a flaw, it has to be something hidden—like a belly button that's an outtie instead of an innie—because trust me, I've studied her as closely as art historians have studied the *Mona Lisa*. I probably know more about her face than she does.

Amber looks up and glances around my room. My mom and I redid it a few months ago with stuff from Anthropologie, changing it from white and boring baby blue to hot pink and orange—not Mom's first choice, but she caved. We gave away the twin-sized bed and replaced it with a double that's covered with a pink-checked spread and pink and orange silk pillows. We bought new wall-to-wall carpeting and a double dresser that looks like a locker, which I think is very cool. And in an East Side boutique, we found a lamp with a shade made of orange feathers.

The room is immaculate now. I vacuumed and hung up the Mount Everest of clothes on my desk chair so Amber could sit if she wanted, but like me, she prefers the floor. I'm about to quiz her on the first word when she looks directly at me.

"How come you didn't tell Meyers I didn't show?" She studies me, almost challengingly.

I shrug and leave it at that. She looks back at me for a full minute, starts to nibble at the corner of her fingernail, then seems to catch herself and stops. Is this a test? Do I get points for not immediately ratting on her? Her blank look doesn't give anything away.

"Convivial," I say, steering the conversation back to schoolwork, the only topic I feel comfortable with.

Amber just stares. "Sociable," she says finally, leaning forward. "Fond of feasting, drinking, and good company." A moment later, she bursts out laughing.

I stare back blankly, taken aback by her abrupt transformation. Then all the coiled-up tension spills out of me too. I start laughing with her, and neither of us can stop.

EIGHT

The next day after school my fingers carry me back to The Swan. I look for posts from my virtual BFs, Melanie and Katrina. Melanie has put up some before-and-after pictures of girls that show killer improvements. Katrina posted an essay from a girl who swears that the surgery is equivalent to a head transplant.

"I'm a different person now," the girl writes. "For the first time in my life, I like myself." I'm about to keep opening links when the phone rings.

"My dad said I could invite you to this unbelievable screening tonight, right after he finishes work," Jen says. "You have to come."

Jen gets to see every new movie made before it opens because her dad is a big-deal producer and the movie companies have screenings for company execs and the press before the movies open to the public.

"It's called *Heartthrob*," she says before I ask. The star is a to-die-for actor who was discovered working as a carpenter in LA. She reads me the entire press release. "I am so psyched."

More than anything, Jen and I love to watch movies. Sometimes when she stays over, we have marathon movie nights and watch two or three without taking a break. Only now, she's on her own.

"I can't go."

"Why not?"

"Mentoring."

"So just reschedule. This is supposed to be such an amazing film, Allie. You have to come."

"I can't reach Amber. I don't have her cell number." Even if I had it, I'd feel guilty about blowing her off so I could see a movie. Jen's annoyed. I hear it in her voice. It feels like we're fighting, even when we're not.

I try not to think about missing the movie while I wait. I check email, fix my hair, dab on more blush because my skin absorbs it like quicksand, and then put away things in my room. At that moment, my mom pokes her head in.

"Way to go." She holds up her thumb.

My mom tries to act cool, but when she tries, it comes off as totally not cool.

The neatness actually annoys me. Every top is folded and put into a drawer. Every shoe is paired on the shoe rack. So that Amber doesn't think I've canceled my day to straighten up for her, I open a shoebox and dump out a pair of shoes, then toss a skirt and some tops on the back of the chair.

I take out the vocab list: hauteur, writ, laudatory...Definitions, using them in sentences, even though you totally never will. Unlike most of the kids in school, I don't have trouble with grammar. Is that nature's way of making things up to me—like the blind person with a sharper sense of smell? Thoughts like that actually cross my sicko mind.

Most of the kids in the class just don't get it. When Mrs. M. gave back our last tests, I heard that Amber got a D, and so did Josh, David, and half a dozen other kids.

The clock now reads five after five. Soooo, this week she's not as prompt. I start homework, and when I look up again, it's twenty after five. Then five thirty. I slam my book down and jump up, nearly toppling my desk chair. Now I'm the total idiot because how could I not have seen it coming? Jen was right. I should have bailed on Amber. If I can still reach Jen, I'll cab it to the screening.

"Hi, it's Jen. I can't come to the phone now, so leave a..."

She's already at the theater and her phone is off.

So I'm double screwed. No movie, and Amber stood me up again.

I take shoes from the closet and throw them across the room one by one, aiming at the model on the cover of *Vogue*. Strangely, I'm comforted by the boom that each shoe makes as it hits its target.

"What are you doing?" my mom yells from the living room.

"Nothing."

"Well, stop whatever you're not doing," she yells back.

The phone rings as if it was prompted by my voice. First I hear traffic sounds, horns and sirens. Jen? Maybe it's not too late. I wait a few seconds for the noise to die down.

But it's not Jen.

"Allie?" Her whispery voice. Amber's outside on a street somewhere. I'm tempted to hang up. I can hardly make out what she says next. After the fire engine goes by, it gets quiet again.

That's when I hear her crying.

NINE

I can barely hear her on the phone. "Where are you?"

"Listen…I just couldn't get there."

Amber-speak for an apology.

Most people who make an appointment actually show up, I want to say. But I don't, because Amber Augusta Bennington has her own behavior manual. Even if she doesn't care about college, doesn't she care how she does in school? How can you not at least try?

I'm freaked by Amber crying.

"Are you…okay?"

"Do I sound okay?"

That seems to set off an even bigger wave of emotion. I'm not sure what to say so I'm quiet for a full minute. "Do you want to come over?"

Silence, and a muffled "Yeah." Then the line goes dead.

Amber stretches out on my bed as if she belongs there. There are tiny, dark water stains on the orange silk pillow under her head. She's been lying there for a while, and we haven't talked much.

Being around Amber splits me into different people: the curious me who wants to understand her. The impatient me who doesn't want to wait to hear what's bothering her. The resentful me who doesn't want to know what her problems are, because what can I do?

The jealous me who wants to steal her looks, but keep my own life and brain.

How can somebody with your looks be unhappy? If I had her nose, nothing else would bother me and the world would have a level playing field.

I look over at her. She hasn't moved. Will she fall asleep? Does she expect me to know what's going on?

Amber must sense something about me that makes her tell me things I have no business knowing. She takes my silence for acceptance, or at least not disapproval. I'm not sure it's either. It's more like wait and see.

Does she trust me, or is it just that she doesn't have anyone else to talk to?

I saw a report on TV that said most Americans have few really close friends, no more than two, and very few, if any people, to confide in. I thought most people were surrounded by friends they could talk to and I was the only misfit. What I can't understand is, if everyone needs love and closeness, why is it so hard to make friends?

Like me, maybe Amber's in the group that doesn't have people to talk to. That would explain why she sits up and leans closer to me.

"My mom's sick...She's bipolar," she whispers like a confession. *Do you know what that means?* her eyes say.

I've heard of that. It's not good, I know, but I'm not sure what it is except that it has something to do with flip-flop mood swings, like PMS, only a hundred times worse. "What does—"

"Her brain's screwed up," she blurts out. Her face darkens. She studies the fabric of my comforter cover really intently, then lifts her head.

"Sometimes she's up and completely manic, cooking and shopping and staying out twenty-three hours straight with different friends. Then she crashes and is so down she doesn't even get out of bed."

"Does she take medicine?"

Amber rolls her eyes. "Just every day. Only sometimes she forgets—or doesn't want to because she hates the stupid little pills with all the power over her—and then that's it. She flips out."

"What about your dad?"

"He travels a lot." She stares out the window, then flashes back to me. "He can't stand to be around her anymore." Her eyes tear up again.

"I'm...I'm sorry." Her sick mom, her dad...I can't imagine what it would be like. "So who...who takes care of you?"

"I take care of me," she snaps back as if I've insulted her.

"But who makes you supper or breakfast...?" I can't help thinking how my mom makes me toast or cereal every morning before school and always has something for dinner, even if it's only takeout.

"I'm sixteen," Amber says like she means thirty. "I can make breakfast, supper, or whatever. Can't you cook a hamburger or buy yourself pizza?"

Amber drops her head and reads from our textbook. Is she really reading or just pretending to? Maybe she needs a time-out from talking about everything. Or she's just tired of talking. Or thinking.

She looks so different now, as if I'm seeing her through a kaleidoscope and with one tiny turn, all the shapes and colors collide, forming a whole new picture. Still a beautiful one, a perfect ten, but now she's more than that.

"Why were you crying when you called me?"

"Feeling sorry for myself." She shakes her head slightly. "Sometimes it looks like everybody else in the entire universe has it easier than I do."

"You just don't know."

"What?"

"About people. What's in their heads."

"Yeah," she says.

My stomach starts growling. "Are you hungry? I'll ask my mom if we can call for pizza."

Amber reaches for a tissue and dries her eyes. "Yeah," she says. "I haven't eaten all day."

TEN

After talking to Mel and Katrina for a couple months, I suggest that all of us meet.

Katrina: I'd love that.

Melanie: Me too. In the city?

A: Let's meet before any of us does anything. And then after.

Melanie: Cool.

Katrina: Winter break?

Winter break—two weeks off—a vacation from school and mentoring. Amber's going skiing with her dad while her grandmother comes from out of town to stay with her mom.

Finally, I'll get to meet Mel and Katrina in person. I have pictures of them in my mind, but I know they're going to look different because all I have to go on are their sketchy descriptions.

Unlike everyone else I know, Melanie and Katrina don't have their pictures up on Facebook. That's the second thing we have in common. I have a caricature of a girl up and I've posted pics of my favorite bands, but none of me except for one of my back in a pink bikini.

Melanie has a collage of faces, only none of them are hers. Like all of us, it's a kind of a *Where's Waldo* of our hide-and-seek lives. I flash back to Amber. A collage of faces would suit her too. Now that I know her—at least a little—it's sometimes hard to pick out the real Amber, if there is just one.

Katrina posted photographs she took of places without people at all—a beach landscape with thick, black clouds in the sky, a forest at night lit by the blinding headlights of a car, and pictures of the dogs at the shelter where she volunteers.

"I'm going to start fostering dogs," she said, "so they don't have to live in depressing shelters while they're waiting for new homes."

Melanie sounds more interested in things than people or animals. But aside from who we are offline, our lives feel bound together after only a couple of months.

With shopping as the excuse, we agree to meet at Saks. After buying presents, we'll eat lunch in the store. It's a short bus ride from our apartment on the Upper East Side, but for Mel and Katrina, it's a trip of more than an hour and their moms have to drive them.

Nobody seems to mind, though, because they'll get to see the Christmas tree at Rockefeller Center, something everybody remotely close to Manhattan feels compelled to do during the holidays. We all check how the latest Norway spruce, lit with twenty-five thousand lights, measures up to the ones we've seen every year before, as if we remember.

Katrina, Mel, and I are talking on a conference call about how we'll recognize each other, and then we laugh when I say the obvious: "Just follow your nose."

✂ — — — — — — — — —

On the day we're meeting, I walk along crowded Fifth Avenue to Saks. Everyone's loaded down with gifts for family and friends, anticipating good times ahead of them. All that cheer should be infectious, but it has the opposite effect on me. I think of what Katrina said: *What we want can't be wrapped up and put under a tree.*

I enter the Fifth Avenue entrance of Saks and the heavy door nearly slams on me. The man in front of me is oblivious. *Am I invisible?* My eyes tear up and I take a deep breath. *Stop it, Allie,* my inner shrink says. *Don't feel sorry for yourself.* I do that a lot—

have talks with myself like I'm a life coach trying to make her client feel more self-confident, more whole. Sometimes it works, at least for a while.

I push my way into the store. The main floor is mobbed this time of year so we picked the Chanel counter as our meeting spot. I'm disgustingly early. I can't help it. I play with the makeup, starting with rose-colored blush.

"Can I help you?"

I look back at the saleswoman. "Just looking."

She walks off to help another customer, and I dot some blush on the apples of my cheeks and check the mirror. Worth blowing what it takes me an entire night of babysitting to earn? Pretending I'm studying the color, I examine the proportions of my face in the mirror.

I read that psychologists took computerized pictures of faces and then played with the proportions, adding or taking away a smidgen here or there to alter the width of the face or just one feature, or to shrink one whole area or another. Then they asked outsiders to not only rate the looks of those people, but also describe what kind of people they imagined them to be. Surprise, surprise, the faces that had been altered to look more attractive got higher niceness ratings.

What stuck in my mind were the tiny differences between faces that got high marks for beauty and those that didn't. Often these came down to fractions of difference in the size of features or proportions—negligible, rice-grain-sized differences. But if it was your face and your so-called life, those miniscule differences could change the tilt of your whole world.

I'm jarred from my thoughts by a tap on my shoulder.

"Allie?"

It's Katrina, I just know. She's even prettier than I imagined. Tall, slim, shy smile, inky blue eyes, and the stick-out cheekbones you see on models. A tiny gold cross dangling from a delicate chain rests in the hollow of her neck. The first thing I think: *Boys will fall for her instantly.*

I look without really looking at her nose and the little flat ridge in the center—as though the bone didn't heal right. It looks strange, unnatural. I see why it bothers her. I give her a quick hug and we look for Mel.

"I'm glad we found each other," Katrina whispers.

"I know. The store is huge."

"I mean out of the whole world," she says. She takes a cookie tin out of a shopping bag and pushes it into my hands. "For you."

"That's so sweet!"

"They are." She laughs. "They're chocolate chip."

I take a small gift box out of my bag and hand it to her.

"Allie!" she says. "You didn't have to."

"I wanted to." I laugh.

She opens the box and takes out the hoop earrings.

"I love them," she says, slipping them through her ears. "Thank you so much!"

I hug her like my best friend even though I hardly know her. She looks away shyly. It's okay, I want to say. I'm not sure why.

✂----------

Before Katrina and Mel, there was no one I could open up to about how I felt about myself. No one who would think I was sane if I obsessed about my nose. No one who could really identify with the thoughts I had that no one else had. I do things with Jen, but we don't really talk about our inner selves. It's mostly about school and other people—how they act and what they wear—or about how we love losing ourselves in movies and pretending we're living in other people's worlds.

We fantasize about actresses and gossip about celebrities and the way they are, but Jen's not a person who lives inside her head. She's also not someone who forgets compliments and dwells on insults.

"You can have different friends for different things," my mom once said. "There are people who hold your hand when you go ice skating and others who hold your hand when your emotional life is on thin ice."

Mel, Katrina, and I live miles apart, but when we talk, we share the same air.

"Nothing I say or ask sounds stupid to you guys," I told them.

"If we were eight years old, we'd be pricking our fingers with needles and mixing our blood," Mel said, laughing.

✂----------

Before I say anything else to Katrina, a girl with a full head of long, brown ringlets comes up to us with a grin on her face.

"I know you're Allie and Katrina."

Mel is a lot like I imagined her, just a little shorter and heavier. Her cheeks are pink from the cold, and her wide smile shows off her straight, white teeth and her signature Clinique Tenderheart lipstick. She radiates energy and confidence. Almost reflexively, I envy her for that. I check out her nose. A bump like mine, but her nose is a little wider. We laugh and hug, feeling happy but embarrassed as if we're meeting at a camp reunion, even though it's the first time we're face to face.

I give Mel her gift—the same earrings I got Katrina, but with tiny blue beads—and she gives both of us small red boxes. Inside each one is a gold rolling ring—real gold—made of three intertwined rings.

"Omigod," we say in unison.

"Note the symbolism, ladies," she says in an exaggerated voice, as if we could have missed it. "The three of us, intertwined?"

We all laugh. I can't believe she bought each of us gold rings.

"My mom was like, who are you really meeting?" Mel says. "I had to tell her fifty times it was two other girls my age, not—who knows who she imagined."

"I had to tell my mom the truth, that I wasn't just meeting

two other girls, but that you were both going to have your noses done too," Katrina says. "My mom is crazed about me talking to strangers online."

"I just told my mom I was going Christmas shopping," I say, starting to feel like I was scheming behind her back. We stand there with people pushing past us and make small talk about the Christmas break, the crowds, and how we love to shop.

"So let's hit the designer floor," Mel says finally. Like baby chicks we follow her to the escalator. She's like a homing pigeon with internal radar.

Not counting the YSL scarf I found at a thrift shop a year ago, I've never owned anything designer in my life, so I feel like an alien wandering around the designer floor. I can't imagine wearing any of the really cool labels. But Mel obviously can. She's into clothes way more than me and can rattle off the names of stores in LA where the stars shop—even though she's never been there—and if you talk about the last Academy Awards, she can recite "who" everyone wore.

"If there was an SAT about designer clothes, you'd get 2400 and go to Harvard," I say.

Ignoring the raised eyebrow from the saleswoman, the three of us lug armfuls of clothes into the dressing rooms, trying everything from perfect black dresses to strapless gowns.

"What do you think?" Katrina says, standing outside our dressing rooms. She should love herself in that black satin halter dress, but she doesn't.

"Wow," Mel says, peeking out from behind the curtain.

A minute later she slinks out like a vamp in a black knit dress by Donna Karan. She's wearing it with the four-inch heels they leave in the dressing room so you don't have to judge how a twenty-five-hundred-dollar dress looks with running shoes or trot out like a dork in bare feet. The dress has long sleeves and it clings to Mel as if it were sewn around her because it's part spandex.

"I feel totally hot," Mel says, strutting over to the three-way mirror and studying herself. She looks at her profile with one finger covering the bump on her nose. I grin because it's something I do, but only in the bathroom with the door closed.

"Ta-da," she says. "The new me."

"Cool." I can't think of anything else to say.

I don't recall ever looking at myself in the mirror and feeling much hotness, though. More like tepid on a good day. But that's just me. I'm sure every time Amber Augusta Bennington glances in the mirror she basks in whatever Mel is now in the throes of.

Mel changes back into her jeans and tosses the dress over her shoulder. When she takes out her credit card, I try not to act surprised. I'm about to take off the orange Tory Burch pants and the sequined cashmere cardigan I've been playing dress-up in. Never mind that the pants fit better than any others I've ever worn in my life and look perfect with the heels I can't walk in.

"You have to get that outfit," Mel says. I shake my head in disbelief. Katrina immediately understands.

"Uh, nooo, I don't think so," she says, "unless you move the decimal point two places to the left."

"Thrift store, anyone?" I say.

Mel holds up her hands as if we're pointing a gun at her. "Sorry, I'm spoiled. I admit it."

After she pays for her dress, we take the escalator up to the restaurant, and the hostess shows us to a table.

"Could we move to a table near the window?" Mel says. We follow the waitress across the entire restaurant to a better table, get settled, and study the menus. There are a thousand choices.

"Shrimp salad and tea," Mel pipes up in a nanosecond when the waitress comes by. "Same," Katrina and I peep in unison.

When the waitress turns her back, Mel smacks the table with the heel of her hand. "So, ladies, I had my consultation."

"Whoooaa, with who?" I say, grabbing the sides of my chair.

"Robert Jordan."

He is *huge*. Doctor to the stars. Everyone who reads *People* knows his name.

"Get out. That's unbelievable."

Katrina is wide-eyed. "How did it go? What did he say?"

"First, I waited in this amazing white office on Park Avenue," Mel says, her voice barely above a whisper. "White silk couches, white orchids everywhere, low lighting, and every fashion magazine in the world. Two other women were also waiting, and we all pretended not to look at each other, even though we were all trying to figure out why the other ones were there. Twenty minutes later, this gorgeous blond nurse called my name."

Katrina's in the moment. "And then?"

"After I waited for about ten minutes in a small office studying myself in a little mirror, he came in with a file folder in his hand." She clears her voice. "He sat down on a stool and looked at me. 'Hello,' he said." She erupts into a burst of nervous laughter.

"Just hello," she says, making a loopy face. "He didn't stare at my nose or do anything to make me self-conscious. He just smiled and looked directly into my eyes and said, 'What can I do for you?'"—she holds her hands out helplessly—"just like that.

"I thought he already knew—duh, from the forms that took me like an hour to fill out—so I pointed to my nose and told him I wanted to get rid of the bump." She pushes her hair off her face like she's reliving it. "He asked me when I made the decision, a little about myself, and then he examined me."

"What did he do?" Katrina asks.

"Looked at my nose from every side," she singsongs, "and asked me whether I had any breathing problems or allergies, my health, blah, blah, blah—and theeeennnn, about five minutes later, he said very matter-of-factly that he could help me." She makes a motion as though she's slicing the bump off her nose.

"It'll be a lot like it is now, just smoother, straighter, and a little narrower, but not tiny," she says like she's parroting the doctor's words. "That wouldn't go with my face."

"What about Mark?" Katrina says, bringing up Mel's boyfriend who can't deal with the surgery.

Mel looks like she's blanking on his name. "I didn't even tell him I had the appointment. I can't live my life for someone else." She shakes her head from side to side decisively. "If he can't live with it, that is so his problem."

Katrina high-fives her. *"Yes."*

"What happened next?" I ask.

"We saw the appointment secretary. I told her I wanted to do it as soon as possible, and she penciled in a date. She gave me the name of the photographer they use who takes medical photographs, then she talked to my mom about money, and that was it."

Mel turns to me expectantly. "What about you, Allie?"

I let out a breath I didn't know I was holding. "I haven't talked to my parents yet. I'm not sure they're going to go for it, but I'm waiting for my dad to get his raise after the first of the year. Then I'll sit down with both of them."

Mel turns to Katrina who shakes her head. "I haven't done anything yet either."

We wait, but she doesn't go on.

"What does your mom say?" I know her dad doesn't live with them.

"She wants me to have it," Katrina says, sliding the rolling ring back and forth over her knuckle. "She feels…guilty."

She sees the questioning look in my eyes.

"My nose broke in a car accident," she says. "My mom was driving. It was her fault."

"Katrina, I'm so sorry…"

"Girls," Mel says, breaking the awkward silence. She puts her hand out to the middle of the table. Katrina put hers over Mel's, and I put mine on top.

"Strength in numbers," she says. "I don't know what I'd do without you girls."

It's like camp before color war when we chanted: "All for one and one for all, united we stand, divided we fall." Only this isn't color war, it's surgery. We're not in camp; we're in an elite club and Mel is the leader.

Just then the all-smiles waitress posts herself at the table. She puts down a small plastic tray with our check and three pieces of candy wrapped in gold paper like miniature Christmas presents.

"Take your time," she says. "Whenever you're ready."

ELEVEN

After what seems like a one-minute winter break, we're back at school. Only now girls are wearing new cashmere hoodies, gold chains, diamond studs, and Uggs in the color du jour. Notebooks are stuffed into designer bags. Mel would fit right in.

All of the teachers seem determined to recalibrate our heads so they're back in work mode. Mrs. M. is more gung ho than ever about the mentoring, hoping the kids with bad grades will relate better to kids their own age than to her—not to mention that the C minus kids are probably eternally grateful to her for springing them from lockdown lunches listening to her tutorials.

In the corridor I see Florence Singer talking to Josh. He should be thrilled that he got the smartest girl in school to tutor him, but his face says that's not how he sees it. Florence looks like she's trying to show him something he did wrong on a test paper, but he's glancing around, embarrassed that someone might see them together.

At the end of the day I leave the building and meet up with Jen. We start to walk instead of taking the bus.

"How's mentoring Miss Perfection?"

"She's got all these problems. Her mom's sick…" I don't go into the details. I feel like I shouldn't give away everything she told me.

"Who doesn't have problems? At least the world treats you better when you're gorgeous."

"I'm not so sure about her."

"Allie."

As we get to the corner, a black Lexus stops at the red light. A minute later Amber runs over and gets inside. Jen elbows me. "Poor Amber," she says.

✂ - - - - - - - - - -

As soon as I get home my cell rings. Text from Mel: Surgeon's office called. Cancellation. Don't have to wait for summer—yeeaaah for me! On for third week in January. Can you believe?

I can't. I can't. I can't. It might as well be me instead of Mel. My heart is racing.

I text back: So fast! Are you freaking?

She responds: Yes!

Mel's the road warrior, I tell Katrina. She took the plunge.

I know. She refuses to let anything get in her way, Katrina says.

I tell her: I'm jealous. Mel's so decisive about everything, so sure of who she is.

Aren't you sure? she asks.

About some things, about my nose…but not my life.

✂ ----------

Mel's pre-op pictures are in two weeks, she messages me later on Facebook. Like horrible candids. So close up they show every vile pore. He shoots you front, sides, and profile so the surgeon can study your face before he operates.

The next step is the lab work to rule out problems that would complicate surgery. Mel's surgery will be in the doctor's office, not in a hospital. I'll rest for a couple of hours until the anesthesia wears off, and then my mom will take me home.

Her nose will be taped up and protected by a splint.

At least it's winter, so you can hide under a scarf. Anyway, you're lucky you live in a private house so you don't have to get strange looks from people in your building, I say.

LOL. There was a girl in my school who went to class with her face all taped up, Mel says. She totally didn't care what anyone thought.

I don't think I could be so in-your-face with it.

I don't know, she says. That's one way to deal with people making fun of you. You let it all hang out.

I call Katrina later that day.

"I can't believe that next time we see her, she'll look totally different," she says. She tells me about a girl from her school who had her nose done last year over Christmas.

"How did it turn out?"

"Aside from bruising around her eyes, she looked good when she came back, except her face looked stiff, almost as if her nose didn't belong to her yet."

I try to imagine seeing a new face in the mirror. How long would it take to get used to? I know the mind takes its own time with changes. People who lose weight say they still feel they're living inside a fat body. And people who've lost a limb feel like it's still there.

"What if you still feel self-conscious after you have the surgery?" I ask Katrina. "What if your old feelings never go away?"

"The old you fades away," she says. "After a while you won't even remember what you looked like."

Then the unspoken: Who's next, you or me?

That night at dinner I bring up the surgery.

"That's not a decision you make lightly," my dad says.

"I know."

My mom takes her fork and starts randomly pushing her

food around her plate as if her response is hidden somewhere under the mashed potatoes.

"Maybe you're being too hard on yourself," she says finally. "You're an attractive girl."

"I could be more attractive if I had my nose done."

We all sit there staring at the food like we forgot what to do with it.

"Let's give it some time," my dad says.

I immediately call Katrina after dinner.

"My parents apply the same rules they use for buying a new car to considering my surgery. It would take an evaluation by *Consumer Reports* to make them okay with it. Then they could analyze size and appearance, American and European models, even trade-ins."

"Ever think of doing stand-up, Allie? Anyway, I'll probably have it done before you do," she says. "I want to get it over with so I can move on with my life."

"Omigod. What will we talk about after the surgery?"

"Daaahling," Katrina says like she's a Swedish film star. "We'll talk about how very, very perfect we look and how extraordinarily happy we are and will be forever and ever."

I inhale deeply from an imaginary cigarette. "Oh yes, *totally.*"

TWELVE

"What are you doing?" Mel asks, keys clicking.

I know what she's doing while we're talking on the phone—shopping online.

"Studying for my oral."

"Excuse me?"

"My parents aren't cool like yours so I'm getting ready for our sit-down." I tell her about my blue-lined index cards and how I use a black gel pen to take my notes under the heading of "rhinoplasty."

She gags. "It's such a horrid word. I mean, how can you not think of 'rhinoceros'? Is there a less appealing animal if you had to pick one to be?"

"What is it with nose words, anyway?" I say. "How can you not barf at proboscis? I mean, who invented that, a lawyer who wanted to make fun of a big nose with a word no one would understand?"

"I never heard of proboscis," Mel says. "Thank God."

"I will be facing a kind of oral exam. They'll bring up the risks. They'll ask, 'What's wrong with your nose?' 'You're a healthy girl,'" I mimic my dad saying. "'Why would you want to do something like that?'"

"Maybe they'll cave," Mel says impatiently.

I can't count on that, so I prepare. I make columns with a ruler: length of operation, recovery time, and how long until back at school. The risks are mostly minor. I don't go there.

Unless I'm prepared, they'll dismiss the whole thing as some "fly-by-night idea"—as my dad calls anything he sees as impractical—as if it's a new fixation of mine. He'll think that all he has to do is wait and I'll get over it and move on to something else I desperately want, like the newest iPad.

My dad takes comfort in numbers, and I found out that more kids have their noses done than any other operation. Last yearly count, almost 35,000 teens had their noses done.

A major deal for us is money. We're not rich. We don't go to a beach house for summer weekends or to Vail for skiing over Christmas. I don't buy designer clothes like Mel. And even though I go to camp every summer, it isn't easy for my parents to pay the tuition, which is close to what the surgery costs.

Katrina calls and I put the cards down.

I tell her about the time a famous writer visited our class and sat in the back listening to us discussing a short story.

"We were all trying to sound smart as we analyzed the plot,

the writing style, the characters. He must have had it with our boring discussion because he stood up and yelled out, 'But what did you think of the story? Did you like it? How did you feel about it? I want to hear about how passionate you are,' he said, 'because if you don't feel strongly one way or the other, nothing else about it matters.'"

"I have to let them know how I really feel and not get caught up in the dry facts."

"If you really want it," Katrina says, "they'll know."

"The decision is easier for you," I say. "You weren't born with a bad nose. It was caused by the accident."

Once it's fixed, she can put all the bad memories behind her.

THIRTEEN

My mom peeks over my shoulder. I'm reading *Vogue*.

"Why are you reading about perfumers?"

"I have to give a speech for Mr. Scott."

"On?"

"He kind of left it open."

"So what are you thinking of?"

"Uh, noses? I don't know. Listen to this: 'Noses are artists-technicians who specialize in creating new fragrances. While there are over a thousand perfumers in the world, there are fewer than fifty expert noses. What separates noses from everyone else? Their extraordinary powers of detection and memory. Noses can identify and remember up to three thousand different smells.'

"Amazing, right?"

She nods.

"Every perfume factory uses perfumers and the main school is in Grasse, France. Every great nose is either a native of Grasse or has worked there in one of the perfume factories, it says." I stop. "Do you think noses have bigger noses?"

"I doubt it," she says. "But I'm sure you could find out."

We talk about how I could pass around different perfume samples and see if kids can smell, say, ten different scents and remember them all.

"It'll be interesting to see if some people have better scent memories than others," my mom says. She goes into her bedroom and comes back with some sample vials of perfume. "You can use these."

I've changed my mind by then. If I dared to do a speech on noses, everyone would call me "the nose who's a nose" or burst into hysterics over some nose joke for the rest of my life in school—and David Craig would find a way to take a picture of me with a bottle of perfume under my nose. I opted for self-preservation.

"I decided on something else."

"Oh," she says, disappointed. "What?"

"Baking a strawberry cake."

She scrunches up her nose. "Isn't that a trifle sexist?"

"No, I'll make a spoof out of it. It'll be funny. I'll wear an apron and pretend I'm a 1950s housewife, making fun of the stereotype of women in the home. Instead of perfume samples, my props will be cake samples—small squares made with chunks of strawberries and iced with strawberry cream."

"Okaaay," she says.

Whatever. It's harder to laugh when you're stuffing your face.

⸙- - - - - - - - - -

No matter what you talk about, getting up in front of the class isn't easy. The whole world stares at you. The tiniest mistake triggers a room full of laughter targeted at—drum roll—you. It's like they want to laugh at you, need to really, so that when it's their turn, everyone will already have picked enough targets of derision and they'll be spared.

So here's what I do: In addition to the apron, I put on a CD from the 1950s of Rosemary Clooney, a famous singer from then (and George Clooney's aunt), singing "Come On-a My House." (No, not totally my idea. I saw a documentary about Rosemary Clooney, and it seemed like such a joke to add the song.)

I walk tall because I've become a character and I can act. I'm alive, pumped up. Allie Johnston has been replaced by a walking, talking, comical robotic wife who holds out a freshly baked strawberry cake like an offering. I watch the class; they're with me.

Maybe I can do stand-up. Maybe I need to.

Everyone laughs, but not at me.

It must be my lucky day.

⸙- - - - - - - - - -

Despite what is going on in her home life, Amber Augusta Bennington has studied the vocab words. We had a test last week, and when she got her paper back, I looked at her. In an instant, I knew she'd gotten a good grade.

How?

She didn't hoist her fist in triumph. Nothing obvious like that. I didn't even see her face light up. She didn't smile or do anything that someone looking at her might see. But since I am an expert on everything Amber, I knew.

What she did do: she glanced at her test, and a moment later, she folded it in half and slipped it inside her notebook. Because I watch her so closely, I know that since the school year started, Amber has never put a test into her notebook—never cared enough to save even one. What she usually does is ball them up and send them shooting across the room on the way out of class. Almost unfailingly, she hits a bull's-eye into the teacher's wastebasket. Mrs. M. never fails to notice, but Amber never seems to care.

Even though I'm getting to know Amber, I still feel awkward around her. Sometimes I have to think up things to say just to fill the silences. Before Amber, the last time that happened was when I was ten and a boy I liked kept calling me for help with homework. I wanted to keep him on the phone longer, so I made up lists of things to talk about.

When we're in my room after school that afternoon, Amber takes out her test paper and holds it up.

I high-five her. She gives me a half smile, and then stares off.

I recognize something troubling in her face. "How's your mom?"

Amber turns to me from the window and shrugs. She has a blank expression on her face.

"Do you want to go over the other work now?" I say finally.

She sits on the edge of the bed and I sit facing her on my desk chair. "Whatever."

I take that as a yes, and for the next hour I play Mrs. M. and go over grammar and usage. I make up sentences and see if she can complete them correctly.

Mrs. Jones complimented Jane and (me, I) on our report.

And on and on.

Amber answers robotically, like a perfect score doesn't make a difference to her. All I see is the cool, protective face she habitually wears, the one I always took to mean she didn't care about anything beyond whether it was a good hair day.

"Do you want to stop?"

Her eyes cloud over. She looks at me, but she's a million miles away.

"Are you okay?" I get up and walk toward the window. What is going on with her? Then I feel guilty and turn back to her.

"No," she says, shaking her head slowly. "I'm not okay." She looks directly at me, her bottom lip quivering. "My mom tried to kill herself," a disembodied voice says. "There was blood everywhere...I got home just in time."

I drop onto my knees in front of her.

"Oh God, what did you do?" I say, my own voice shaking.

"Called 911...I rode with her in the ambulance to the emergency room. I had to wait outside while they took her in and stitched her up." She looks down at the floor like she's outside the ER again.

"Then what?"

"Finally they let me see her." She shakes her head. "She was so pale. Almost lifeless. She already looked dead to me."

I cross my arms over my stomach. I can't imagine how it felt for her. I should feel the sorriest for Amber's mom and all her problems, but the one I really pity is Amber. I keep looking at her, trying to figure out how she's coping with all this. She slides down to the floor and buries her head in her hands.

FOURTEEN

I almost wish she hadn't told me. I can't get it out of my mind now.

How does she go through the day with a family drama like that? What does she do for diversion? Shop? Hang out with Josh? Even sleep with him?

Until now, Amber has been a blank slate that I measured my fantasies of happiness against. I always saw her like the actresses in the magazines who look like they live in a perfect bubble. Fame, great looks, money. But then one day you find out all their pictures were retouched, and when you pick up the next month's magazine, you see the paparazzi shots of them heading to rehab, their faces drawn, hiding behind big sunglasses, hair tucked into baseball caps.

The curtains around Amber are parting now, and the girl I see has a life that's a world away from what I imagined. I think of a sentence I heard in a play: "The only normal people are the ones you don't know very well."

✂ - - - - - - - - - -

I rush off to school, trying to stop the film in my head of Amber in my room telling me, but it seems to start over and over again like a movie trailer that's stuck.

Jen once told me that to manage her scattered life, she taught herself to compartmentalize.

"What do you mean?"

"Decide what your priorities are," she said. "Worry about things when they need to be dealt with, not before."

"I'm not sure how to do that."

"On Monday, I study for the math test I have on Tuesday. And Tuesday I focus on my sched for Wednesday. Why agonize over something a month away if you're powerless to do anything about it now?"

That made complete sense to me. It was so focused, so I attempt that now. On today's priority list is Mel's surgery.

When my clock radio went off at six ten to a miserable weather report about scattered showers, I lay back in bed with the covers pulled up to my neck. All I could think about was what she was about to go through. I feel like I am her fairy godmother who will wave my magic wand and make it all go okay because right now, Mel's life is intertwined with mine. She is my alter ego. If things go well for her, that will be a good omen for me.

Now she's already in her car. At seven a.m. she'll be at the surgeon's office, face scrubbed, wearing a shirt that buttons down the front so it doesn't have to be pulled over her head after surgery. She'll be in the recovery room one to two hours later. After the anesthesia wears off, her mom will drive her back to Connecticut. Mission accomplished.

I'm going through it with Mel. I am in her head every step of the way. So is Katrina. This is group surgery—one nose, three brains.

"You have to swear to call me and Katrina as soon as you're home," I said to her last night.

"Swear."

"You *swear* you swear?"

"I swear I swear."

I think back to then.

✂------------

I was in bed about to turn out the light. I went to Facebook one last time to check for messages, but there was nothing new. Before I turned off the lamp, I grabbed my cell to turn it off. Just as I lifted it, it went off in my hand. I jumped.

Mel.

"I thought you'd be sleeping by now."

"I can't sleep."

This wasn't the upbeat, goofy Mel who coasts through life thinking about clothes and things she's "dying to do."

"Are you okay?"

A few seconds went by. "Allie?"

"Yeah?"

"Remember when we once talked about whether we ever thought about something bad happening…like during the surgery…"

"Yeah."

"And I said I never thought of things like that?"

I waited.

"I was lying."

I held my breath.

"I'm really scared," she said, starting to cry. "I mean, what if I die?"

"You don't have to worry. You just don't," I blurted out like I knew. "Everybody gets scared, really. I go to the bulletin boards all the time, and everybody feels that way," I said, even though it wasn't true.

"Yeah?"

"Absolutely. And you know what?"

"What?"

"You're going to not only be fine, but you'll also look so gorgeous that Katrina and I will totally hate your guts."

"You think?" She sniffled. I knew I made her smile.

"Yes, so just go to sleep and think about the gorgeous girl you're going to turn into in less than twenty-four hours, okay?"

"Okay," she said. "And Allie?"

"What?"

"I love you."

"I love you too, Mel. Now go to sleep and call me tomorrow."

"I swear."

"You swear you swear?"

"I swear I swear."

I was about to hang up when I heard, "Allie?"

I pulled the phone back up. "Yeah?"

"Something we all have to remember. It's all in the name of beauty," she said like a solemn oath.

"Uh, yeees," I said. Then I hung up. Beauty? Just beauty? Was she serious?

FIFTEEN

Jen and I hang out and eat sushi while we watch a new film about a rock group. She has an amazing apartment on Park Avenue with a den that they turned into a screening room with couches with footrests.

"I'm glad you came over," she says, turning to me after the movie ends.

"Me too. We haven't done this in so long. I've been so busy with mentoring and my own work that I don't have a life."

"You hang out so much with Blondie now that we never do fun stuff anymore."

Blondie, Jen's new name for Amber. She doesn't like to say Amber's name because it means acknowledging her existence.

"I have to mentor her."

"Forever?"

"Until she passes the tests, at least." I put on my coat and stand outside her door waiting for the elevator.

"Maybe we can have a sleepover next week," Jen says.

Only next weekend I'm supposed to see Katrina. "Definitely, but the weekend after is probably better," I say as I step into the elevator.

"You're so busy," she says as the doors close between us.

✂------------

It's almost six when I get home from Jen's. I didn't tell her about Mel. It sounds stupid, but on some level I felt like I'd be betraying a trust. This is something Mel, Katrina, and I were going through. Jen isn't part of it.

I lift the phone at six thirty to check for a dial tone because it's been totally dead. Not even a market research company calling to do a survey. Katrina's also sitting by her phone.

"Did she call you?"

"No."

"I'm going to call her."

"Do you think you'll be bothering her?" Katrina says. "She's probably sleeping."

"So her mom will answer."

It rings three times and no one answers. I call again. Still no answer, then the message. I hang up.

Where could she possibly be? I call Katrina. I need to vent.

"You don't not come home unless something is wrong," I start after her hello. "You remember the article about the girl in New Jersey who died?" It was a story that ran in Katrina's local paper.

"Ugh, yeah."

"I mean, it doesn't happen often. The chances are miniscule, but sometimes…" I don't tell her about Mel's call. Did she sense something? Was that why she was afraid?

"Nothing's wrong," Katrina says. "Everything gets delayed."

"Nothing's wrong," I repeat like a mantra. "It can't be. It can't be. It can't."

"Mel's healthy, and she has a great doctor," Katrina says like she's weary. "He works on celebrities and models. Famous people who are on television," she says, like that proves something.

"Yeah, his patients have surgery over and over. That's why they look like they do. They don't die. Bad things don't happen to them. I'm being stupid," I say. "I have to stop inventing stuff. Stop assuming the worst."

"Don't even acknowledge that something bad could happen because you're putting it out there," Katrina says.

We hang up, and six becomes seven.

A long, concerned look from my mom across the dinner table. "What's wrong?" The textbook-sized rectangle of lasagna in front of me is almost untouched. It repulses me. I push it away. This has never happened.

I shrug. "I'm not hungry."

I'm glad I never told her that Mel was having surgery this morning. My parents are the last ones I can talk to about what

I'm feeling now because they'd immediately lapse into "I told you so" mode. And if something bad did happen, forget surgery for me.

I go into my room. The world is suddenly in slow motion. Maybe something is going on that I don't know about, and that's behind why she didn't call. Maybe the phones are out in Connecticut because of a fire. Storms. Traffic.

Eight.

Eight thirty.

I turn on the TV and lie back in bed. A long, boring report about the expanding waistlines of Americans. I must have drifted off to sleep, because my body jerks when the phone rings and my chest lunges to life with kettledrum heartbeats.

"Allie?"

A weak voice that sounds like it's coming from the bottom of a well. *"Mel?"*

"Yeah." It's a sleepy, drugged Mel on speaker sounding like she has the worst cold in the universe. "Everything went fine."

"Great!" I shout. "I want to see you."

"No, you don't. Ugh, blood." She spits.

"What?"

"It drips out," she says. "That's normal, they said." She spits again. I hear her working hard to draw in a breath through her mouth. "I am definitely not ready for my close-up."

"But you will be!" My attempt to be reassuring.

"I'll have to remember that."

"Do you hurt?"

"Sore," she says, "but not pain pain."

"I'm just *so* happy to hear you're okay. Katrina and I were literally out of our minds."

"Thanks, Allie," she says, yawning. "I'll call you tomorrow."

I speed-dial Katrina. "Not to worry. She's totally fine. She just called me."

"I knew she'd be," Katrina says.

"So did I. Piece o'cake."

SIXTEEN

Back in school, it's a relief not to be thinking about Mel's surgery. Only now I'm in Mrs. M.'s class and there's one empty seat in the last row.

Her absence is as dramatic as her presence.

By now I should have realized that Amber Augusta Bennington is nothing if not unpredictable. Just when I thought she was starting to act normal, she morphed into the Amber of the locker door, staring into the abyss, famous for throwing curveballs.

I've been helping her for a month, but never mind that she was supposed to come over after school. She didn't even let me know she wouldn't be in school. I overheard Mrs. M. telling Amber's history teacher that Amber would be "out indefinitely." It has to have something to do with her mom, but there's no way for me to find out for sure. Even though Amber lets little bits of her life trickle out, her private life stays private.

The only person who might know what's going on is Josh. But I've never said more than two words to him. Why would he tell me anything?

At lunch, I'm at my regular table with Jen. She's talking to a girl in her class about a history test, which segues into a discussion of grades and—no surprise—Amber. It's as though there's a magnetic field around her, and eventually everything is drawn to it. Or not a magnetic field, a black hole.

"Josh said she got a ninety on the last English quiz," Jen says. "I don't believe it, do you?"

"She's smarter than I gave her credit for."

"If she's so smart, why was she failing for half the semester?" Jen says. "She needs help."

I shrug. "Maybe failing was her way of asking for it."

SEVENTEEN

*A **train runs*** from Grand Central to Westport, an upscale town in Connecticut on Long Island Sound. Katrina's mom drives her to my house. We take the subway to Grand Central, and then we'll take the train to Mel's. I pass on breakfast. I can't eat when I'm nervous.

"Do you want to stop for a muffin?"

Katrina shakes her head, touching her stomach. Kindred spirit.

It's been three weeks since Mel's surgery. Luckily, she didn't have much black and blue. Makeup that's heavy enough to hide bruises will pretty much cover the little discoloration that's left.

"Email us pictures!" I said. "We're dying to see you."

"Come up here," she said. "I want you to see me in person."

Mel's brother Matt picks us up at the train. We can't miss

the fire-engine-red Mustang he's leaning up against territorially, arms folded over his chest. He's three years older than Mel and a freshman at U Mass. He's home visiting for the weekend.

Matt's tall with thick, curly dark hair and Mel's warm brown eyes. He looks like he lifts weights. My cheeks start to warm. "How could she not have told us about him?" I try to tell Katrina with my eyes. Luckily it's cold outside so I have a reason to look flushed.

He walks toward us. "Allie and Katrina?" My hand automatically shoots up to my forehead to fix my bangs. Pretending the sun's blinding me, I reach for my sunglasses to cover the bump. It's sunny out so it won't seem like I'm trying to look cool.

Despite the freezing weather, all Matt has on are jeans and a black crewneck sweater. After he slides into the driver's seat, I open the side door and nudge Katrina. "I know," she mouths back before climbing into the back.

He is totally hot.

It doesn't escape me that there's no bump on his nose. He does not need fixing.

After a few minutes, he pulls into a circular driveway in front of a white brick mansion with a big porch and a view of the water. Katrina and I exchange looks.

"So how does she look?" Katrina asks as Matt fumbles for his house keys.

"Kinda good." He shrugs. "Different...I don't know."

Katrina laughs. "Are we even going to recognize her?"

Matt smiles. He eyes Katrina like he likes her. "She just had her nose done," he says playfully. "The rest of her is the same."

He looks over at me and says teasingly, "So you both gonna have it done too?" Then he seems embarrassed and tries to catch himself. "I just mean that Mel…" He shrugs. He's backed himself into a corner.

"It's okay," Katrina says, giving him a lopsided grin. "And definitely yes." I nod, eager groupie number two. He shakes his head and looks skyward as he opens the door.

Mel's parents have done a serious job of decorating. Every piece of furniture is upholstered, but not just with one kind of fabric. Every couch and chair is covered in two or three contrasting fabrics with fringes and strange trims that twist and pucker. There's hardly room to sit because small, fancy pillows are everywhere.

The living room floor is covered with a wine-and-blue floral-patterned carpet with a leopard border. Thick blue velvet drapes puddle on the floor like the train of a wedding dress. The lamp shades are like Easter bonnets with fringe. On top of a coffee table there's a stack of big, expensive books, the kind that nobody ever reads, about sailing ships and Russian art. A long, winding staircase goes upstairs, probably to Mel's room and the other bedrooms.

"*Mel!*" Matt shouts. He waits. No answer. He goes halfway up the staircase, makes a megaphone with his hands, and yells again, a trace of annoyance in his voice. A moment later she walks out to the top of the staircase. She's wearing the black Donna Karan dress with high heels. Her arms open out to the sides theatrically. "Ta-da."

She spent an eternity on her hair. It shows. It's long, layered, wavy, glossy, perfect. She could pose for a shampoo ad. She struts down the staircase, making her dramatic entrance. Katrina and I are bug-eyed.

Prom queen. Poster girl. A magazine-perfect Mel who told us ahead of time she was having her makeup and hair professionally done for our visit and had killed herself losing seven pounds on some new low-carb diet. Her eyes are lined and shadowed with smoky brown-black powder so they look dark, sultry, and enormous. Her eyebrows are perfectly arched, starting and ending where they're supposed to, the way they show you in the magazines. Thanks go to a woman who worked for Lancôme who lives near Mel and makes house calls when people have special occasions. For Mel, this is as special as it gets. I'm waiting for fireworks to go off on the front lawn.

She looks way better than I imagined. Katrina and I take it all in.

But as I stare, I start to have an odd feeling that I'm growing guilty about having.

Here's what I'm asking myself:

She looks amazing, but why? Is it the new nose or is everything else she did just as important, maybe even more important? I can't help the guilty thought that the surgery hasn't changed her that much.

I know it's not supposed to. All the surgeon did was take off the bump and narrow her nose. If his work is good, the new nose fits the face so well that you shouldn't focus on it. The idea is to improve on nature, not radically change it, so it should be hard to pick out what's different.

To throw people off, some women change their hair color or style right after surgery. That way, people who see them credit the new hair for the improvement. Something like that is going on when I look at Mel. Better, but why? I thought I would see more of a change. Like a detective trying to nail down a suspicion, I wish I could see before-and-after pictures of her with the old nose and the new, both with the same perfect makeup and her hair done this way so I can really see the difference.

"Here's what I hate," I once told Katrina. "When you see before-and-after pictures of people who had plastic surgery, and 'before,' they make sure they look their absolute worst by not wearing makeup and pulling back their hair so it's completely unflattering. Then 'after,' you see not only the surgically fixed face, but also the perfect hair and makeup so they look doubly better."

"It's totally unfair," Katrina said. "You can't compare the pictures."

But Mel isn't thinking what I am.

The girl who was unhappy with herself has vanished. This

one is in love. With herself. She's glowing, living proof that in addition to plastic surgery, feeling beautiful goes a long way toward helping you look that way.

"Oh, Mel!" Katrina says.

"You look soooo good," I add.

Mel hugs us. When she steps back, I see the slightest blotches of yellow underneath the makeup.

"Thank you, thank you, thank you. I can't believe it, I really can't." She turns and stares at herself in a gilded full-length mirror by the front door. "When I think of all the years I hated how I looked...ugh." She lets the sentence trail off.

"How does Mark like it?" Katrina asks.

"He's history," Mel says, waving him away.

Then Mel's mom comes in and introduces herself. She's tall and slim. No wonder Mel had no arguments from her. If there ever was a family nose, there's no trace of it now.

Mel takes our hands and leads us into the kitchen. I've never seen one like this before. It's massive. The island in the middle has a brass pot rack over it that holds a matching set of maybe twenty-five gleaming copper pots. There's an industrial-sized stove and a dining table that could seat twelve people in front of an enormous fireplace.

I turn back to Mel. I don't want to stare, but I can't keep my eyes off her nose. Katrina is also fixated on studying her. Mel doesn't miss the fact that we're examining her like she's a lab specimen.

"You're making me self-conscious!" Katrina and I laugh. We sit down at the table and help ourselves from a big platter of sandwiches—chicken salad, shrimp salad, roast beef, turkey, and roast vegetables—that Mel's mom must have ordered for us.

"I hope I end up with such a perfect nose," Katrina says. "Can I photograph it and show my doctor?"

"No." Mel puts down half of her sandwich and shakes her head emphatically. "You can't do that. It's like asking the surgeon to turn you into somebody else, and you don't want that. Dr. Jordan told me that girls come to him all the time with pictures of movie stars, asking him to give them the same noses." She shakes her head. "That is so completely ridiculous."

We go up to Mel's room after lunch. For the rest of the afternoon, she walks us through what happened after the surgery. She used bags of frozen corn to ice her face and reduce the swelling, she says. She had little sponges in her nostrils that made her nose itch.

"I couldn't breathe," she says. "I hated that part."

Getting used to your new face must be a big adjustment, because for the entire afternoon she's never far from a mirror. Katrina makes fun of her.

"Are you checking to make sure your new nose is still there?"

"You'll see," Mel says.

She shows us her new collection of NARS and Chanel makeup,

gives us old stuff she's hardly used, then models new clothes in her walk-in closet. We move on to talk about hairstyles, and she shows us pictures she's collected because now she's thinking of changing her hair.

I glance at my watch. "If we want to make the four forty..."

Mel jumps off her bed and we all hug.

"I am sooo glad you came. I don't think I could have gone through this without you." She goes over to Katrina and squeezes her shoulders.

"You're next, missy. I can't wait until you join the club."

Katrina smiles and rolls her eyes. Mel walks us down the long, winding staircase. She's wearing a different dress and shoes now. Katrina and I are in jeans, down jackets, and Uggs, our bags bulging with Mel's old makeup and T-shirts she didn't want anymore. We wave good-bye and get into the car with Matt. He puts on a CD and blasts it, turning to me at one point.

"The group is called Panic Stricken," he says, even though I didn't ask.

"I never heard of them."

He laughs. "They go to my school."

I'm glad I didn't pretend I knew the music. I can tell he's in love with the sound because of the way he thumps the steering wheel with the heel of his hand in time to the music. Nobody talks, and he pulls up to the station just in time.

"Thanks," Katrina and I say almost in unison as we fling

open the doors and bolt for the approaching train. Matt just nods without missing a beat.

EIGHTEEN

Amber Augusta Bennington's absence from school doesn't give me a free ticket out of mentoring. Her progress proved to Mrs. M. that I could do the job—and that I was better at it than some of the other mentors. So her Plan B.

Like during a square dance where you're perpetually changing partners, I am given someone new to lock arms with: David Craig.

I'm not sure what happened with his mentor and actually don't want to know. What I know for sure is that he is not coming to my house. If I went to the bathroom, he'd probably steal a look through my underwear drawer and shoot pictures of my thongs.

I'm not sure why David feels the need to perpetually carry his camera. Maybe the real world isn't weighty enough for him. As for the eyeliner thing, by now most of us ignore it because we know how desperate he is to get attention.

So déjà vu all over again. I tell him to meet me in the library.

"Got something against Starbucks?"

"It's just easier to stay here," I say. He mutters something under his breath and walks off.

While I wait for him after school—textbook out, pens lined up, notebook open—I can't help flashing back to the first time I was supposed to meet Amber. Suddenly I feel sad all over again about what she's going through. I don't know where she is now. What I do know is that she disappeared from school more than halfway through the year so she'll miss classes and her grades will go down again.

Her mom tried to kill herself, and Amber came face to face with that.

How can she live with that? Can she keep all that grief and helplessness inside herself without imploding?

I think of how she looked lying on my bed, so still she didn't seem alive while tears dripped from her eyes like from the dolls you fill with water so real tears seem to spill out of the little holes in the corners of their eyes.

A heavy textbook drops on the desk in front of me and I jump.

"Wake up," David says.

Is startling someone lost in thought an amusing thing to do? David must think so.

"I'm up." I say, glaring at him.

He sits down at the table, sliding his camera out of his

pocket and strategically placing it next to his notebook as if it's as indispensable as a pen.

"This is English, not photography." My low and controlled voice.

"You have to be ready," he says. "You never know when the perfect picture will appear in front of you."

I give him a long, bored look. "Oh…I get it."

"What is it with you?" he says, as if he tasted something sour. "That attitude."

"Excuse me?"

He screws up his face. "Why are you so uptight?"

"Being your mentor isn't number one on my list of fun things to do, okay?"

He works on looking bored. "I'm a fast learner."

I don't mention his grades. I open up our grammar and usage book. He gave me his old tests so I can tell what kind of mistakes he makes. I come up with sentences, right and wrong.

He isn't all that impressed with the need to know it.

"I'm not gonna write books," David says, as if that explains it all.

"And your point is?"

"Why is this important?"

I tuck a strand of hair behind my ear and lean toward him. "It's important because these are the rules of the English language, which you should know whether you choose to follow them or not."

I think of the high I get when I've aced a test I've killed myself for. The validation, as if the universe is saying that if you work hard enough, you can get what you want.

He glares at me like I'm a freak. A second later he narrows his eyes.

"Don't move."

He lifts his camera and studies me through the lens. It feels like bullets are flying.

"Do you mind?" I turn away, the legs of the chair scraping the floor like a scream.

"What?"

"We're supposed to be doing grammar, not taking pictures."

"You don't like yourself," he says matter-of-factly.

I close my eyes and shake my head slightly. "What's that supposed to mean?"

"I can always tell." He puts the camera down.

"Thank you, Sigmund Freud."

"The camera doesn't lie."

I close the book and start packing up. I can't deal with him. I just can't. I tear off a slip of paper and jot down the pages we were supposed to go over.

"See you next week. Make sure you study."

He shakes his head. He's pissed off? Maybe in the future, I should be a tad nicer to him. Otherwise, he may snap my picture and who knows where it will end up.

NINETEEN

I don't know how I have the nerve, but I stop Josh Ryan one afternoon when I see him searching behind the perfectly weathered, brown leather bomber jacket hanging in his locker.

"Josh?"

He turns and raises his eyebrows as if he can't imagine what someone like me would want with him.

"I…I just wondered…"—*I'm almost stuttering, now isn't that cool*—"if you knew what was happening with Amber."

He looks back at me, deciding whether he should blow me off.

"She's out of town."

He starts to turn back to his locker. I'm dismissed. "Do you know where?" There's something behind his jacket on the shelf under his textbooks that he keeps reaching to get. After he pulls out what looks like an address book, he faces me. Close up, he's got not only the softest jade green eyes that exactly match his T-shirt, but also smooth, tanned skin and wonderful lips. For a millisecond, I wonder what it would feel like to be kissed by those lips or loved by someone who looks like that. Really, he's the personification of hotness.

If his face weren't enough, he's about six two. Josh is the male equivalent of Amber. Classically perfect, at least outside. Poetic justice, really, that the two of them hooked up.

"I just feel bad for her," I say, going on more than I thought I would, but something about his hesitant expression seems to invite that. "I know she's having problems and...and I was helping her with her homework so she told me about her mom."

"She's in Cleveland with her dad," he says finally. "He's trying to get her mom into treatment in some clinic there. Amber couldn't stay home alone so..." He holds a hand out in a helpless gesture. We both stand there for a minute, not saying anything.

"Is she coming back? I mean she...she lives here."

"She wants to...but I don't know."

"Do you have a number for her? I never got her cell."

"I don't know if she wants to talk to anybody," he says, shaking his head.

I get the feeling that "anybody" might include him. I stand there for a few seconds, shrug, and start to walk away. Then I turn back to him. "Listen, could you tell her I asked about her?"

I open my backpack and jot down my cell number on a scrap of paper. "If she wants to call me, give her my number, okay?" He looks at it and nods.

Somewhere in the middle of history class, I think of Amber's expressionless face, her vacuous stare in the picture that's still on her locker door. No one can tell what she's coping with. You can't glean any insights into what's going on in her life. It's all hidden away behind her eyes. And then it hits me that my own picture might show the same empty stare with no clues to the life behind it.

✂ - - - - - - - - - -

I'm psyched because it's Friday and Katrina's spending the weekend with me. I rented movies for tonight, and tomorrow I'll show her the stores where I like to shop. I told her I'd take her to the cool resale stores on the Upper East Side where you can find amazing clothes for half of what they'd cost in department stores. We might go ice skating in Central Park too.

When I brought up skating, Katrina said, "I used to wish that I'd fall and break my nose so I'd have a reason to get it fixed right away."

"But that would kill!"

"It kills now," she says.

After dinner, Katrina and I have a three-way call with Mel. She hooked up with John, a hottie from a nearby school. Was it the nose? Does surgery pave the way to instant popularity?

"I didn't have a social life before—unless you count Mark, which I really don't," Mel says.

We hang up and watch movies. Now that Mel's had the surgery, our little group has been whittled down from three to two.

Mel's the graduate.

Katrina and I are still facing the final.

She has seen one surgeon, but she didn't feel comfortable with him so she has an appointment with someone else. Her mom can't afford a Park Avenue doctor, so they'll use someone closer to home or in the hospital where her mom works. Katrina's mom is a nurse in the pediatric ICU.

"Some of her patients are hand-sized preemies with breathing problems," Katrina says. Some were born addicted to drugs because their moms are. Then there are older kids who fall off slides or swings and land on their heads.

"Doesn't all that sadness make her depressed?"

"You put up a protective wall," Katrina says, like it's simple. "You have to." She reaches for her black and pink LeSportsac and pulls out Victoria's Secret PINK pj's. It looks like she's staying for a month because she packed all the clothes she wants to show me.

"I'm a shopping addict," Katrina says, laughing. "Only my budget is like Mel's on a starvation diet."

That's okay because, like me, she loves to search through vintage and resale stores for odd, cheapie skirts and tops that other people have passed over. Then she thinks up retro looks that no one else would imagine. She likes to reinvent herself every time she gets dressed. Being tall, thin, and blond definitely works to her advantage.

After we look over each other's stuff, she shows me a new T-shirt she's never worn. It's got lace around the collar and along the edge of the sleeve.

"It's sooo nice."

She tosses it over to me. "Take it. It'll look great on you."

"But it's new. You never even wore it."

"So?"

I want to give her something new from my closet in exchange, but she shakes her head. "It's fine."

We tug open the futon for her and make the bed. It's after twelve.

"I'm not even tired," she says.

"We can talk in the dark," I say, even though my mom will start innocently poking her head in if she hears us before she goes to bed. With the blinds tilted up, we're both silhouetted in the darkness.

"I always wished I had a sister I could talk to and share a room with," Katrina says. "I hated being alone."

"I used to want a sister or brother. But now I like getting all the attention."

She doesn't answer.

We talk about the surgery. "I can't imagine what I'll think about after I have it, when the nose issue is gone," I tell her.

"For me, life is divided into before and after," Katrina says. "It's like I'm not living these days. I'm just putting in the time until I have a different nose."

"You know what my grandma always used to say? 'Don't wish your life away.'"

"What did she mean?"

"I was telling her I wanted the week to be over because I had a hard test coming up. She said to live in the moment and be thankful for every day you have and not wish your time away."

"Well, there's a part I'd like to wish away," Katrina insists. "The 'this nose' life."

"What if after you have it done, it doesn't change you so much inside? What if even with a better nose, you still feel like the same person?"

"It'll change me," she says like she knows.

"How do you know?"

"I just do."

I hear her yawn. "You tired?" I ask.

"Not really...I only sleep about five hours a night. If I go to bed early, I just lie there."

"I sleep nine hours, sometimes more." Next to Katrina, I'm Miss Average American Girl. Married parents, not divorced. They're both teachers. With so many kids with divorced parents at school, being normal is the new abnormal.

Katrina's life is like Amber's. Katrina never talks about

her dad or her parents. Amber doesn't say much either. Little puzzle pieces of their lives come out, but the whole picture never seems to become clear. Sometimes it's as if they're scared for you to find out who they are, so they hold so much toxic stuff inside.

We talk about college. I'm not sure where I want to go. "I'm thinking of staying on the East Coast so I won't be too far from home and I can visit, even on weekends."

"I want to go to California," Katrina says. "I'm applying to Berkeley to study psychology."

"It's a long trip back."

"I don't think I'll come back," she says. "Once my nose is fixed, I want to leave this part of the country altogether."

"Have you ever been to California?"

"No."

"So how do you know you want to go there?"

"I saw pictures," she says. "It looks pretty."

I hesitate. "Won't you miss your mom if you're so far away?"

"I want to have my own life."

I wonder if I should I ask her about the accident. My voice grows so faint that I barely speak the words. "I...I don't really know what happened when you broke your nose."

Seconds go by and she doesn't answer. Maybe I shouldn't have asked.

"If you're going down a road at night and the car coming at you has their brights on, it blinds you," Katrina says finally. Her voice sounds distant, almost disembodied. "My mom works the late shift so she's always tired."

A wailing car alarm outside steals our attention. It grows louder and wider, taking over our consciousness like the shrill cry of a baby that can't be ignored. I want to open the window and hurl something at the stupid car.

Katrina waits a few seconds and then goes on. "We were coming home from a neighbor's," she says. "My mom was picking me up after work."

"Allie?"

Blinding light floods the room as the bedroom door is flung open, interrupting Katrina again. It makes me squint.

"What?" I nearly jump off the bed.

"You girls are still up?"

"Sooo?"

"Please go to sleep." The door closes as quickly as it opened. Neither of us says anything.

"Katrina…"—my voice trails off—"I really care about you, and I feel like I don't know you…and your past."

She doesn't answer and we sit in the dark. "I hope you don't mind that I said that…"

"It's okay."

Is she going to answer?

"Allie…I wasn't in an accident," she says finally, her voice changing.

"What do you mean?"

"That's what I tell people because I don't want to get into it."

"Into what?" An ambulance siren gets louder and louder as it races up the street, sending a wave of fear up my spine.

"My mom did work on the late shift all the time, and she was never home at night," she says. "She got paid more money to work late and we needed it." She stops and waits. "Allie... this is something I never told anybody. I put it in my diary, but I couldn't..."

I'm aware of needing more breath and try to hide the sound of me taking it in. I wait for her to go on.

"My father used to drink," she says. "I smelled it on his breath all the time after dinner. And one night...when I was ten, he came into my room." She exhales again. "I don't know if he was lonely because she was never around, or he was just crazy or something. But he got into bed with me...and there was nothing I could do about it."

"You mean he..."

"Yeah."

Everything around me starts to feel unsteady, like what they say you feel during the first rumblings of an earthquake when you've lost your bearings. You're not sure if it's you or the ground beneath your feet that's trembling. All you know is that you're off balance, out of sync with your surroundings and unable to reach out to something that will steady you.

"Oh God, Katrina, I'm so sorry."

"When you're ten years old, you're confused about

everything," she says. "I was so scared and I felt so powerless. It was horrible, Allie."

"You never told your mom or anyone else?"

"She wouldn't have believed me anyway," Katrina says. "She always said I lived in a fantasy world. Anyway, he told me not to say anything. He said I'd be sorry if I did because I could never come home again."

I feel sick in my stomach. "Why?"

"He said if I ever told anyone, the police would come and take me away and put me in a foster home...that I'd never come back and see my mom or any of my friends again, ever."

Her voice is hollow, like she's reliving it.

"He said I'd move from home to home in bad neighborhoods because people who foster kids do it for the money and don't care what happens to the kids."

"Oh, Katrina." I press my hands over my mouth. I can't think of what else to say to her. I've never met anyone who this happened to and I feel overwhelming pity.

"Every night I prayed for him to die," she says, her voice flat and lifeless. "It was the only thing that would stop it so I'd be left alone."

I move over and hug her.

She shakes her head. "I can't believe I'm telling you, Allie," she whispers. "But we tell each other everything so..."

I don't know what the right thing to say is, so I just sit there next to her with my arms around her.

"The last night it happened, I fought back," she says. "I just decided I wasn't going to let him do it anymore. He smacked me hard, and I felt something crack. I had a terrible pain in my head. I started crying hard, screaming. Blood was everywhere, all over the bed and the floor."

"What did he do?"

"He got so scared that he carried me into the car and took me to the hospital. He told them I fell out of bed. They didn't believe him. I could tell by the way the doctor was looking at him and asking him all these questions. The whole way back, he didn't say anything. After I went into my room, I heard the front door slam and the car start. They gave me a pill for the pain and it made me tired. I didn't wake up again until the morning. When I opened my eyes, my mom was sitting on my bed and her eyes were red. The phone started ringing and all these people were calling. I just knew."

"What happened to him?"

"His car hit a tree, my mom said. He was killed instantly. I wished for it, prayed for it, but when it happened, I didn't know how to feel. Was it my fault? Did I cause it? I felt sick inside, only I didn't know why."

"When did you tell your mom?"

"A few months later, after we had a lesson in school about sexual abuse. They said the people who do it are usually friends of the family or even people in your immediate family—parents, uncles, or cousins. I wanted to stand up and yell, 'I know, I know.

It happened to me.' I wanted someone to look at my face and realize it. I wanted someone to understand, but no one did. My heart was pounding so loudly, but nobody heard it. After that, something flipped in me. I knew what I had to do. I just had to get up the nerve. Finally I did tell her."

I've heard stories like this on TV, but I never knew anyone who went through it. Things like that have never entered my world. It's as if someone faraway that you read about in a newspaper and don't really think about suddenly comes up and lands in front of you. I think of all the conversations we've had and how I never had any idea of what she had to live with every minute of every day. My mind is veering in all directions, as all my emotions collide. I want to let her know I'll help her in any way I can.

"I'm here for you, Katrina, no matter what."

She squeezes my hand.

I can't help thinking of Amber. Like Katrina, she probably survived her awful home life by trying to escape to another world inside her head. Only with Katrina, every mirror brought back the nightmare.

TWENTY

After the weekend with Katrina, I welcome losing myself in school on Monday. What's ordinary is now comforting. At three o'clock, I go to the library to meet David.

I stop.

I am not seeing this.

What is his story?

As I make my way to the library table, he's studying himself in a small mirror and putting on more eyeliner. I cannot fathom what his makeup thing is about. I slide down into the chair next to his and open my book, ignoring him.

In addition to the eyeliner, he dyes his hair coal black, only I can see his brown roots. It's not that the hair color thing is so strange; I'm just weirded out by the idea that he gets into costume to go to school. But whatever. I guess people have different coping mechanisms. Like wearing baggy clothes to hide fat. Or hiding nose bumps under sunglasses, or stick-out ears under long hair.

"Did you study?"

"Study?" Eyebrows raised as if I've taken him by total surprise. His idea of a joke.

"You know, open book, read words, commit to brain."

"Duuuuuh, *yes!*" He hoists his fist in the air.

"Good." With luck, he'll get his grades up, our mentor relationship will come to a halt, and I will get my life back. I turn to a section on dangling modifiers and slide the book in front of him.

I point to two sentences: "You're on."

Warm and sweaty, the lake water felt refreshing.

Wearing high heels, the long walk to the car was exhausting.

He reads the first one out loud and grins. "The lake water was warm and sweaty so it felt refreshing."

"Funny."

"The lake water felt warm and sweaty, so I felt refreshed."

"Are we done having fun?"

He answers by lifting his camera. Only this time, he doesn't first study me through the lens.

At the first click, I turn my chair away from him.

"You hate your face," he says. *Click. Click. Click.* He's still shooting.

I don't answer.

"What is it, your nose?"

I'm still silent, but that doesn't stop him. Finally, I hear him put the camera down. "I think it's actually a cool nose," he says. "Really. It's an in-your-face, empowering schnoz."

I turn back to him. Is David Craig actually sitting next to me telling me what he thinks of my nose and trying to psych out how I feel about my face?

"How about if you don't bring up my face issues, and I don't get on your case about makeup or hair dye or whatever else it is you need to do to face the world. Deal?"

"You don't want to talk about my bellybutton ring or all the piercings…"

"No." Louder than I intended.

He shrugs and flashes me his signature smirk. "Well, then…" He looks down at the textbook. "The long walk to the car was soooo exhausting," he says, "because I was wearing high heels." He shimmies his shoulders, closes his eyes, and lowers his head.

I take a deep breath and stare at the table, holding back the slightest urge to smile.

TWENTY-ONE

After dinner, I talk to Katrina online. I don't bring up what she told me. It's out there. She'll say something if she wants to. She's put it behind her. So will I. I bring up David and tell her about mentoring him and how he makes me crazed with his camera.

"What is it about being in front of a camera?"

"You're giving the world a permanent picture of what you look like," she says.

"Remember the empty places in the yearbook where they wrote "camera shy"?

"That was yours truly," she says, "I didn't show up for mine."

"I didn't think there was a choice." I always assumed you had to be out sick to miss it. Obviously not. I now find out that other people squirm at being photographed too. Then I wonder. When David wields his digital truth box, is my angst related to him or the camera? I don't trust him. That's part of it.

But it's more than that.

Click. In one hundredth of a second, your face is frozen in time for the world to examine.

But do people actually examine you? Do they care? Or is it all in your head? When we had a sleepover, Mel described something she'd read about called "the spotlight effect."

"You feel like you're walking around with a giant spotlight on you, and you're so embarrassed by what you think people see that you shrink away from living up to your potential."

I took out a flashlight and lit up her face. "You mean like this?"

"Exacto."

Amber's face pops into my mind. She's probably one of the few happy to be in the spotlight. For her it's probably a turn-on to be photographed. The camera loves her. When her picture is being taken, she probably feels like she's being watched by an admirer.

Flashback to the picture on her locker door. I make a note to take a closer look at it. Now that I know her, will I see something I didn't before?

And the pictures David took of me. What did he see? I can't remember the last time I studied a picture of me, so I go into my dad's desk drawer and get his camera. I close the door of my room and hold the camera at arm's length.

Click. Click. Click. Click.

I sit on the edge of the bed studying the pictures, going from one to another, forward and back, knowing I can delete them like a bad sentence, never to exist again except on my mental hard drive.

But I don't.

I try to figure out who this person is. How good or bad she looks. Like a stranger would. Like David.

Is it just the nose, or is there an overall image problem? How much truth can you see through your own eyes?

"One thing's for sure," Mel once said. "Nobody looks at us as hard as we do."

"If I could draw, I would look in the mirror and put down what I see, as if I were looking at myself as a stranger would," I told Katrina. "I'd see shadows, the way light hits the planes on my face, the spaces between the eyes and the nose, the cheekbones, the mouth, the chin."

"Allie!" she said, exasperated. "You don't have to know everything. I mean, you never will."

I want to understand myself better, to see my face objectively, like an architect who studies a building, aware of its strengths and its faults, or an artist who is capturing a face on a canvas and has to know every shadow and nuance to capture it accurately. Looking at pictures isn't enough, but what else I can do?

Katrina answers quickly: "Just live."

TWENTY-TWO

"Josh said you asked about me."

It takes me a second to place the voice. I wasn't expecting Amber to call.

"I was wondering...how you were." It comes out forced. I'm uptight. I can't help it. She must think I'm crazy.

She brushes over the "how you were" part with a pat "okay." Then she moves to what's on her mind. "Are you mentoring someone else now?"

"David Craig." Enough said.

"Eeuuw," Amber says. "He wears more eye makeup than I do." We both laugh.

"Maybe you could help him with his colors," I say.

She snickers.

"He spends more time studying me than the grammar," I say.

"Last year when I sat in front of him, he used to shoot the back of my neck," Amber says in a weary tone.

The strange thing is that Amber is a world away, and we're on the phone talking like we're in the dining hall and she's my best friend.

"So what's happening with you?" I'm watching myself in the mirror as we talk. "Are you coming back to school?" I start snapping pictures of me on the phone with Amber, watching how my face changes as I talk.

"I'm not sure." Her voice goes back to the Amber with problems. "My dad's still working things out here. We can't leave yet."

"But if you miss too much school, won't you get held back?" It pours out in a rush. Even if she thought of it, there's nothing she can do, so why didn't I just shut up and not bring that up?

"Who knows."

"Isn't there somebody here you could stay with in the meantime?"

"My older sister, but I don't know."

I assumed she was an only child. "If you need something from school—homework or anything—I can send it to you."

"Maybe, thanks. I got to go."

I hang up and stare at the phone.

TWENTY-THREE

There are a few dishes my mom excels at. Salmon croquettes, for one. Fried chicken's a runner-up. So Jen comes over for a chicken dinner, partly because she wants to see me, and partly, I think, because of the food.

"Clean up and start the dishwasher," my mom says, leaving us to talk. She's now on some kick about job-sharing in the home.

For the first time, I tell Jen about Mel and Katrina. They're such a part of my world now that I'm starting to feel like I'll be holding half my life back if I don't.

"You met them on a plastic surgery website?"

"Yes, why?"

She makes a face. "That's so strange."

"I'm thinking about having my nose done." There, it's out.

"How come you never said anything?"

"I don't know."

As she stares at my profile as if she's never seen it before, I change the subject from me and tell her about Mel's surgery.

"That's cool," Jen says. "I mean after hating her nose for her entire life, she had it fixed and now the problem is gone."

Without prompting, the next thing I hear is, "I hate my ears. I always have." Even though I've known Jen for more than five years now, I've never noticed her ears. Maybe because her hair completely covers them, except when the wind blows.

She reads my face because she lifts her hair on one side. I see a flash of ear before the hair drops back and covers it. Her ear does stick out a little.

"At least you can cover your ears. You can't cover a nose—unless you live in the Arab world and cover up in public." I take a second piece of fried chicken. I'm about to bite into it, but then stop. "I wonder if I'd still want my nose done if hardly anybody saw it?" I say, almost to myself. Probably. You fix things you don't like for yourself first, not for anybody else. I turn back to her. "You could have your ears fixed."

She makes a face and looks off as though she's thinking about something privately. "When you have your nose done, I heard they break your bone. I mean how gross is that?"

"You don't feel anything. You're totally out." I don't think she hears me.

"I mean…eeeewww." Then she looks at me. "I mean, unless you really want to and you need it, and then, you know, you just…do it…I guess."

TWENTY-FOUR

The empty chair in the back of the room isn't empty anymore. I look and then do a double take.

Makeover. Big time.

The long hair is gone. It's cut very short, almost wispy, pixie style. No one in the universe could wear it that way. Except Amber. The absence of long hair seems to remove all distractions so that her green eyes and perfect nose stand out that much more, highlighting her ethereal beauty. The black, fitted knit dress with long sleeves and black alligator heels don't hurt either. Not exactly a run-of-the-mill school outfit, and everyone notices in a good way. Amber didn't just slip back into school; she made her red-carpet entrance.

For the first time, everyone seems as fascinated with Amber as I am. I look at her and smile. She smiles back. I don't want to gawk like a stupid groupie, so I don't turn around for the rest of the class.

Josh is in the front row, head swiveled around. Too bad the blackboard isn't in the back of the room because then he'd be paying complete attention. I get the feeling he's as surprised by seeing her with the new haircut—or just seeing her—as everyone else is. Amber gets off on surprising people. I think it's her way of testing the boundaries of loyalty.

After exaggerated throat-clearing, Mrs. M. calls on Josh who has been paying attention to nothing other than whether Amber has been receiving the sexual impulses he's been wafting out to her.

"Sorry," Josh says, turning back to Mrs. M. with an embarrassed grin. She fixes him with a long, paralyzing stare before repeating the question. He shifts uncomfortably in his seat. "I don't know. Sorry," he mumbles, rubbing the back of his neck.

"It would behoove you to pay closer attention, Mr. Ryan."

"Behoove?" says a whispery voice from the back of the room. Someone else snickers. Mrs. M. silences the class with her penetrating glare.

When the bell rings, I close my notebook. Amber walks over to my desk.

"When did you get back?"

"Last night," she says.

She's wearing the blank face. Josh hangs back behind her, waiting. His eyes are cast downward, mesmerized by her sheer black stockings and the four-inch stilettos.

"How's your mom?"

She shrugs. "Getting better, I think. They're trying some new medicine."

There's an awkward silence. "Good," I say. "You look cool."

She looks down at her skirt. "My mom's clothes from her modeling days."

Her outfit looks like something Mel would be all over. I expect Amber to turn and go, but she stands there.

"I guess I'll see you later," I come up with. Lame, but I can't think of anything better. She turns to Josh, and as they walk off, he slips his arm around her waist. With her high heels, she's as tall as he is.

When I get home that afternoon, I'm still thinking about Amber and how she looked, and I decide to pretend—like I'm playing charades by myself—that I'm going to be Amber. I am not on drugs, so where did I get the wacko idea to play this impersonation game?

If you think something, you can make it happen, people say. That doesn't mean I've lost it and I think I can turn into an Amber clone. It just means that all of us probably have a hand in the way fate works. We should definitely play all our cards to make things come out the way we want them to, and not roll up into a ball and play dead if our lives aren't perfect.

So like a windup doll, I strut around my room trying to act and feel like someone who's totally okay with herself. And even though I'd never admit it to a living soul, I'm having fun inside the head and body of this new, genetically improved, bionic Allie doll.

I slip on my one pair of high heels and take long runway strides, head held high. Abracadabra, I'm five ten, one hundred twenty pounds, and drop-dead gorgeous. Women all over the planet would kill to be me, Allie Johnston. I whisper my name like I'm a sultry, cover girl. *Allie Johnston.* I change the look in my eyes. I walk with total confidence and sizzling sex appeal. I'm hot, I say to myself, like I'm Mel.

I'm hot, hot, hot, hot, so hot, hot, hot!

You can do this, a smug little voice inside me says. *You can literally become the person you want to be. It's all a matter of the thoughts you put in your head and carry around with you.*

It's up to you! the voice says, like my inner confidence coach, my cheerleader.

I'm strutting from one end of my room to the other, Miss Total Hot-Shit Goddess of the Universe, teen idol, the envy of girls everywhere.

"Dinner's ready!" The door flings open and my mom stands there. Her face shows she does not understand this.

Unfortunately the earth doesn't open up and swallow me.

"I'm rehearsing a part for the school play," I yell like a bomb exploded in me so she doesn't think I'm high. "Would you mind closing the door?"

"Oh." She nods, closing it behind her.

I kick off the heels so they go airborne, disappearing behind the bed, along with the hot-shit goddess with the loud mouth. The person left is the real, lukewarm loser, Allie Johnston.

Or not.

I put on my pink, furry slippers and make my way into the kitchen.

Hot, hot, hot. I laugh to myself. Inside my head this time.

TWENTY-FIVE

The phone rings during dinner. We mostly have a family rule about not interrupting the meal to answer it. My dad goes into his mantra about the phone "disturbing the rhythm" of the meal. Not clear on that one exactly, but that doesn't mean we ignore it. What we do is chew slower and sort of tilt our heads toward the answering machine. Can it wait or not?

One ring. Another. After the third there's a soft, "Hi, it's Amber." I leap for it. My parents exchange looks like, "Do you know what this is about?" I take the phone into the living room.

"Hi," I say back.

"Are we still…you know…still doing the mentoring?"

Interesting that Amber asks that. At some level she doesn't care much about school. Does she just want to hang out with me?

"I don't know." Mrs. M. didn't say anything to me, and I was already saddled with David. "I mean, I could help you if you want."

"Otherwise, I might get Florence Singer."

I am now soaring over the rooftops. Amber has given me a passport to the world of cool people.

"You want to come over tomorrow?"

"Tomorrow's good," she says.

I go back and finish my entire plate full of pasta with clam sauce. My parents are almost done.

"Who was that?" my dad says.

"Amber."

"She's the one with the sick mom," my mom says with a slightly pitying expression.

I nod. "She's back in school now and she's coming over tomorrow. I have to help her with English."

"Do you want to invite her for dinner?"

Amber Augusta Bennington, the girl who I always envied, the snootiest girl in the entire school, sitting down to dinner in my house with me and my parents. How weird is that? The truth is, I never pictured someone like Amber doing something as ordinary as eating.

Then I wonder, when was the last time Amber's mom made dinner for her? Or the last time she had any kind of home-cooked meal? Even a dinner out with her family?

"Yeah, sure." And a moment later. "Do you think you could make salmon croquettes?"

TWENTY-SIX

Text from Katrina the next morning: Found surgeon and I'm good to go. Call you later.

Ten words that unleash a torrent of mixed emotions: happiness, fear, anxiety, relief. In my mind Mel, Katrina, and I are cardboard cutouts from a board game. Mel has jumped to the top and hit a hundred, while Katrina has lengthened her lead on me.

Glad to hear. Talking to my parents this weekend.

Katrina calls after dinner. She sounds so happy. Her doctor is associated with the local hospital. "Even though my nose was broken before, it won't be a problem, he said. I'm on for the week of Presidents' Day in February."

Unlike Mel who had it done in the doctor's office, Katrina

will have her surgery in the hospital. "I'll go home at the end of the day and come back in a week to have the cast removed."

When I get off the phone, I mark the date on my calendar and text Mel. She's online and with her phone every waking moment, except when she's in school.

Cool, she texts back. Will call immediately. Wanna get together in the city again for shopping?

Maybe all three of us? We can toast Katrina before the surgery.

And you? Mel asks. News?

Discussion this weekend. Do or die.

I put a red star on my calendar, next to the word "discussion." I can't put it off any longer.

This time I don't have to wait for Amber to come over. We go home from school together. Jen does an obvious double-take as we pass her at the bus stop. She has a slight frown on her face. Am I violating some kind of trust by helping someone else with English?

"What's up?" she mouths.

"Mentoring," I mouth back.

She shrugs. Her face says she's annoyed. If Amber sees, she pretends she doesn't. Today she's obviously wearing another one of her mom's outfits. I see tiny gold buttons on her jacket with two C's on them.

"You look so cool."

"Thanks."

"How come you're wearing your mom's clothes?"

"She said I should take everything."

I look at her, uncertain.

"She likes to wear comfortable clothes now," Amber says. She hesitates. "She's coming to terms with the fact that she's not a model anymore."

"So that's good?"

"That's what they say." She stares off into the distance. "She was a famous model and she's not anymore...so it's hard for her to, you know, deal with."

"Now she has you."

"Yeah," Amber says. "That's part of the problem."

✂ - - - - - - - - - -

When we're sitting in my room eating Doritos and going over the essay, I look at her while she's writing. Without the long hair, she looks almost childlike.

"Who cut your hair?"

She puts down her pen. "I did. I was looking at myself in the mirror, and the next thing I knew, the scissors were in my hand and snip, snip, snip, I was cutting it all off."

"How come?"

She takes another Dorito. I hear the sound of her crunching it. There's a faint dusting of orange powder above her lips. Either she doesn't know it's there, or she doesn't care. Her face shows she's trying to figure out the answer. "To freak myself out, change everything." She looks at me to see if I get it.

"Head transplant?"

She stares back blankly and then bursts out laughing. "Um, exactly." When she stops laughing, she looks at me.

"What?" I can't read her face.

"I can talk to you," Amber says.

That's all.

We study, but not as hard as when we first got together. Amber's more plugged in to school now. I'm waiting for her to answer a question when she looks up at me and studies me for a few seconds. She rubs the side of her chin.

"You should definitely wear your hair in a topknot."

"You think?"

She comes over and lifts the top of my hair, then pulls out a few wisps on either side so that they land on the sides of my face, softening the look, making it less of a style. "Do you have a hair tie?" I get one for her and she puts it around my hair. She pulls out a few more wisps.

"Go look in the mirror."

I walk to the mirror over my bureau. "Yeah, I like it."

"And you should wear makeup."

"I do but—"

"You can't see it."

She goes to her bag and takes out her makeup case. She

pulls a brush out of a snapped, plastic case and dusts pink blush on the sides of my face. She steps back to look at her work. "You have good skin," she says. Next, she takes out a dark brown eye pencil. After rubbing the end on a tissue, she lines my top and bottom lids and smudges the line with her finger, then nods.

"I'm always afraid of looking too made up." I stare into the mirror. I like what she did, but I have to get used to it. It's me, but more so.

"If you put it on right, it shouldn't look heavy, just smoky."

I turn to Amber. Should I say what's on my mind and has been from the first second I saw her? I settle on, "Want to trade faces?"

"You have a different look," she says offhandedly. "So you should go with that."

That's the hugest compliment I've ever gotten.

Then the words just come out of me. "I'm having my nose done," I say.

Matter-of-fact, no big deal. I can't believe I told her, but I know Amber won't make fun of me. And she won't react like Jen and make a face like the whole idea is repulsive and I'm pathetic. Amber cocks her head slightly. Plastic surgery is no big thing to her, I'm sure. Models have their noses done all the time.

"There's an Italian model I know who has an unconventional profile," she says. "That's why they hire her. Shock value, I don't know…She doesn't fit the mold."

"What would you do? Would you live with something you didn't like about yourself?"

"I get off on changing my look all the time. You make people focus on what you want them to." She stares off. "That's why I like modeling. You're always reinventing yourself. It's like acting."

I expect her to go on about wearing red lipstick to draw attention to your lips, or putting on dark shadow to highlight your eyes. "But surgery," I say. "Would you go that far if you didn't like something?"

Her face darkens and I know she's not thinking about things like fixing a nose. "There's no surgery to fix what I don't like," she says. A moment later, tears well up in her eyes.

TWENTY-SEVEN

David Craig stops me in the hall outside English. "Can you come to my house after school for mentoring? I have to go home to let the dog out."

I won't run into anyone there. And it's not like I'm afraid of him, unless he attacks me with his camera. The truth is, the last thing I want to do after a whole day at school is hole up in the library.

His brownstone is on West 82nd Street near Central Park. As I walk up the steps to the front door, the first thing I see and hear is a dog. He's standing on his back legs, leaning against the door, and barking as I wait for David to open it. He's black and shiny—a Lab, I think.

"Okay, easy, Horace," David says, holding on to the Lab's collar as he opens the door so the dog doesn't jump on me. After sniffing me, Horace immediately rolls onto his back.

"He wants you to scratch his stomach," David says. I smile at the way the dog's back leg moves back and forth like he's running in place when I scratch him. "Horace, after the poet?"

David shakes his head. "After the school. We were driving up near Horace Mann, and we saw him wandering around the street. No collar or anything. It was cold and he looked pathetic, so we took him home with us." He shrugs. "We named him after the school."

"Maybe he's a graduate."

"Not likely. He flunked out of obedience school." He looks at me straight-faced. "Maybe you could mentor him."

"Funny."

He smiles. "C'mon," he says, getting to his feet. Horace trails behind us as we go past the front of the first floor, which has a big rolltop desk and floor-to-ceiling bookshelves. Beyond that, there's a living room with a fireplace and a spiral staircase in the corner. Out the window I see a backyard with a table and a barbecue.

David's camera is nowhere in sight when we sit downstairs at the table in the kitchen. Just as we open our books, a younger David clone walks in.

"Hey," he says to both of us.

"My brother, Jesse," David says.

Jesse smiles. He's got good hair. It's shaggy, well cut. He looks shy, approachable. He opens the refrigerator and takes out a container of milk and then reaches for a box of cookies in a cabinet. A moment later he walks out of the kitchen and I hear footsteps going up the staircase.

I go to the chapter we're on. When I look up, it hits me that David doesn't look the same. I knew something was different as soon as I walked in, but with Horace begging for attention, I didn't pay much attention to David. Now that we're sitting together, I look at him and see what's changed.

The eyeliner. His face looks softer, more vulnerable without it.

"You look different." The words spill out of my mouth. Why didn't I just be quiet about it?

A half grin. He doesn't say anything.

"How come?"

"I wash off the eyeliner when I get home."

"And the reason is?"

"Don't you want to get out of your school clothes and change when you get home?"

I nod.

He shrugs.

"Why do you wear makeup?" I suddenly feel I have to ask since we're on the topic. Not challengingly. Just curious.

"To look different."

I shake my head, not understanding. "Why?"

"To freak people out, okay?"

"Well, you've achieved your goal."

He looks back at me with a hint of a smile. Then it's gone.

For the first time, we're having a serious conversation. It's not angry or ironic, for whatever that's worth.

"We should get started." My mom doesn't like me to go home alone after dark, but I don't tell him that. I find my place in the book and we go over two chapters—"Words Often Confused" and then a second one that explains when to use numerals and when to spell out numbers. I can tell he's concentrating. He seems to get most of it.

"Good," I say.

When I look up I can't believe it's almost six. I start to pack up. I have to walk a few blocks and then wait for the crosstown bus. "I think you're finally getting it, which is good news because Amber is back and now I'm helping her too, so I don't have a life."

"She's cool," he says. "*Très cool.*"

Très cool? For some reason I can't fathom, I hear myself asking him if he likes her new haircut.

"She's going through a new phase," he says, not answering the question. "She doesn't want to be the old Amber anymore."

My first reaction is to make fun of him. But I don't, because I think he's right and I didn't see it that way. "Yeah, you're right."

David looks at me intently. I know what he's thinking. I've lost the attitude. It disappeared when he washed off the eye makeup.

TWENTY-EIGHT

"So what are you doing for the weekend?"

Amber shrugs and looks bored. "I have no idea whatsoever."

"Do you want to sleep over at my house tonight?"

She glances at me with a glint of interest in her eyes. "Sure."

I have sleepovers with friends all the time, so having Amber stay over shouldn't be a major deal.

But it is.

It becomes like planning a wedding when all you've ever done before is have stupid little birthday parties. I don't want her to think my family went to a lot of trouble, as if no one has ever stayed over before, so instead of the steak or chicken pot pie that my mom offers to make for supper, I decide we should just go with pizza and have it while we look at the new modeling shots Amber said she'd show me.

Before she comes over, I fix up my room and throw out things like water bottles, price tags from clothes from six months ago, and scraps of paper with vocab words from last semester. In the midst of my frenzy, the phone rings.

"Are you up for a movie?" Jen says.

"I can't."

"How come?"

"I have a sleepover."

"With who?"

"Amber."

"Oh," she says. Just "oh." It's like she sees herself as a Ford that I've replaced with a Mercedes. I could ask her if she wants to stay over too, but it wouldn't work. She doesn't like Amber, and three is an unlucky number when it comes to friends, especially when one is a new friend.

"See you Monday."

She hangs up.

✂------------

I expect Amber to come with a ginormous bag of clothes. She doesn't. Aside from her portfolio, all she brings are boxers, a T-shirt to sleep in, and a second pair of jeans. Everything is rolled up neatly inside her messenger bag.

After we eat, we look at her pictures. There's one with her hair up in a ponytail with almost no makeup. Another with her in a bathing suit. In a third she's wearing a flowered dress and high heels like she's going on a job interview. Then there's the Britney

Spears one with her in torn jeans and a midriff top with her hair around her shoulders. I'm surprised at how different she looks in each of the pictures.

"A model is like a blank canvas," she says. "They want to be able to turn you into whatever they need."

"I feel like ten different people inside," I blurt out, surprising myself. "Like I don't know who the real me is."

"Sometimes I don't think there is a real me," Amber says.

"Do you feel like you're different with different people too?"

She nods.

"I wonder if everybody feels that way."

She studies me. "I don't really have friends," she says, "so I don't know what other people think."

"What do you mean?"

"What I mean is, I don't have friends," she says, annoyance creeping into her voice. "People don't want to be friends with me."

"Why?"

She tosses her hair back. "I have no idea."

"They're probably jealous. I mean, you're way better looking than most of the people in the world, Amber."

I've been thinking it for two years, but I never imagined actually saying it to her face. Now, though, there's no reason not to. Amber needs to know it. Strangely enough, I don't think she does, which makes me like her more.

"They don't know me," Amber says. "They wouldn't be jealous if they did."

"Well, I know you and I'm like *totally* jealous," I say like a Valley girl as I make a freak face. Amber looks at me and laughs. She makes her own sick face back, yanking open the corners of her mouth and the sides of her eyes with her thumbs and pinkies. "Yeah, I'm totally gorgeous," she says, and we both crack up.

Her cell phone rings. She reaches for it and looks at the number.

"Josh," she says, rolling her eyes. She tosses her cell back into her bag.

"The best-looking guy in the whole school and you don't answer?"

"Do you know how it feels when someone loves you, loves you, loves you?" she says mockingly, as though it should be obvious.

"No."

She puts her hands around her throat as if she's choking herself. If she doesn't make it as a model, she can be an actress. My laughing encourages her to keep pretending to be choking herself but on a really comic scale.

When we finally stop laughing, I look at her. Suddenly, I feel compelled to ask her something I've always wondered.

"Do you feel pretty?"

She looks at me as if that's a really odd question. "What do you mean?"

"When you look in the mirror. Are you happy, I mean really happy with the way you look? Do you feel good about yourself?"

Concern shadows her eyes. "Do you?"

"Me?" Is she putting me on? I hesitate. I see that she isn't. "Not good, and never pretty. On good days I'm okay with myself and who I am at least, but on bad days..." I just shake my head. I'm my own worst nightmare.

"Well, I feel like a fraud," Amber says flatly.

"What do you mean?

"People think I'm pretty, or whatever, but that's not the person I am."

"But...you look good."

"Not inside," she says.

She grabs the remote and clicks on the TV. We sit there staring at music videos that stream by like mental wallpaper.

Without a word, she reaches for the bottle of melon-colored nail polish and starts putting it on her toes. When she's finished, I take it and do mine.

"It's a cool color," she says.

I hold out my hand and look at my fingers questioningly. Amber takes my left hand and puts on the polish. Then the right. She passes the bottle to me and I do her nails.

"Now we're both pretty," I say like a robotic voice-over.

She blows on her fingernails and smiles. I shake some gummy bears out of a bag and we share them, lifting them with the pads of our fingers and trying not to mess up our perfect nails.

I get giddy for no reason, as if someone piped laughing gas

into the room. The world's not divided into perfect and imperfect anymore. Or happy and sad. Life seems fairer now.

Except for one small thing: her nose.

TWENTY-NINE

I try to remember when we last had a family conference. Last year to decide teen tour versus going back to my usual camp in Maine? The safe sex lecture with all of us looking out different windows? I mean, my parents and I discussing condoms and body fluids?

Maybe "conference" is the wrong word. Meeting? Discussion? Whatever, the three of us sit together in the living room. I've asked for this meeting, but the whole thing feels forced because it's not a conversation around the table or a "how was your day" kind of deal.

My parents have no idea what this is about. Even though I've told them how I feel about my nose, they have no idea how much time I spend dwelling on what's in the center of my face.

We'll talk after dinner because I wouldn't bring this up on empty stomachs. So moving along after roast chicken, baked potatoes, and salad, I help with the cleanup and that is noticed because it is so out of the ordinary. Our kitchen is small, with no room for three of us, so we bump into each other as my father brings in the dishes and stacks them on the crowded counter, while I scrape everything into the garbage, pretending I don't mind how revolting congealed chicken fat looks on the plates. My mom loads the dishwasher, aware that I'd rather be somewhere else. She looks relieved when my dad and I finally walk out. After everything's all cleaned up, we make our way into the living room, sit down, and get uncomfortable.

I look at them both straight on.

"I've put off this discussion for a while, but now I really need to talk to you." I look out the window briefly, opening myself to psychic powers passing through, and turn back to them. I think of "pacing" from speech class and keep that in mind for maximum impact. "Since I was twelve years old, I've wanted to have my nose done…"

There, it's out there.

They don't laugh or snicker. My soliloquy goes on for about three minutes straight, maybe more. I can't even remember because when you're nervous, everything is a jumble. You don't know what you spouted out or if it made any sense because your mouth is trying hard to keep pace with your pulsating brain. You become like a football player running with the ball. All you know is that you can't stop or slow down, because if you do, you'll lose the advantage and get tackled.

I tell them about Mel, how she credits the radically different way she looks and feels about herself to the surgery. Finally, I go through the reasons I want it done, ticking them off one by one, calmly, logically, methodically:

» A change in appearance equals a happier me.

» Greater self-esteem. With the nose issue gone, I can concentrate more on who I am, my sense of self, my schoolwork, looking ahead to college.

I ease into cost. The best doctors. How long the whole thing takes. Plastic surgery is more common than ever. It's part of the culture now, like it or not.

I stop and suck in air. My dad's looking at me. No nervous gestures that shout out he's uncomfortable. My mom can't seem to stop playing with the glass Easter eggs in the bowl on the coffee table, and it's making me nervous. I keep glancing at her nose and then looking away

At least they're listening, and they're not hitting me with questions, objections, risks, and stumbling blocks. At least not yet.

This is not going the way I expected, and the air in the room seems to grow heavier by the moment. My senses are tingling and I feel like I suddenly have supernatural powers so I can hear what's inside everyone's head and read their expressions.

I am coming to the end of stating my case, and I feel the way I do on New Year's Eve when I'm filled with excitement and fear and a total awareness of what's passing and approaching as the last, meaningful seconds of the last minutes of the year are ticking by and I'm counting down louder and louder and crazier, almost holding my breath. Nervous, anxious, fearful, as I welcome in a new era and the baggage of the unknown with it.

In just seconds, when the ball falls, I'll know whether I'll be entering the New Year and new era with a different face, or whether my world will shatter into a million glistening shards when I hear a resounding no and have to resign myself to staying the way I am until I'm old enough to live alone and pay for the surgery with my own money.

My mom clears her throat. Have they been listening patiently because they feel they should, not because they agree, and now they'll begin their full frontal attack?

"This is surgery," she starts. "There's anesthesia."

"I know that."

She holds up her hand. She's not finished. "I realize that more and more teenagers are doing it…It's the thing these days…

The thing?

"But," she shakes her head, "this is a time in your life when you're changing…"

"It's not something I just came up with. I've wanted this for years." My body heats up. I'm breaking into a sweat, losing my cool, despite my resolve to stay calm and act mature, like I'm old enough to handle everything. Everything is starting to crash in on me like a giant wave that's about to take me down. I blink hard to keep the tears behind my eyes. I won't cry. I won't let them do that to me.

She shakes her head. "Being in high school isn't easy, Allie. There's a lot of schoolwork, a lot of pressure to get good grades, to compete with everybody else and look your best and be popular. I know you care about your looks, but if you waited..."

"I don't want to wait," I almost shout. I'm tempted to rush out of the room and slam my bedroom door. I hate when they do this to me. My face is getting hot, blood throbbing in my head. I'm about to answer and let my anger out, but then at the very moment I take in a breath, I detect the slightest change in her face, a shift, an opening. It's like the clouds have parted for just the briefest second and I see a flash of resignation.

Silence.

We look at each other as seconds go by.

"Well, if you're absolutely sure," she says. "If this is something you really and truly want—"

Everything inside me feels hot and electrified, like the cells within my skin are about to ignite into tiny bursts of flame.

What am I hearing?

"—then we'll support you."

I lean forward and my face breaks into a smile.

"*But*," she adds, holding up her hand like a traffic cop. "We want you to really think it through and make sure you're positive, because you'll be changing who you are," she says, "the face you were born with."

"And if I am, if I'm sure…you mean I can do it?"

She glances over at my dad and nods slightly. "It's something we'd rather you didn't do, obviously. But if you're sure…" Her voice trails off.

I sit there for a minute. "Okay," I say, my heart pounding inside me like a tribal drum sending out a message.

And what am I feeling? Happiness, relief, surprise, extraordinary joy. Which emotion is rising to the top? I can't tell because I'm being bombarded.

It's done.

Decision made. I have their support.

I cross my hands over my chest. "Thank you, really."

The amazing thing about parents is how they can still surprise you. They had clearly been over this before. Otherwise they would have been giving each other sidelong glances to find out what the other one was thinking and feeling.

But there was none of that, and none of the pencil pushing—as my dad calls it—when he's trying to figure out whether we can afford something and he's analyzing it. This was a done deal from their point of view. I see that now, only I don't know how I missed it. They were just waiting for me to put it on the table.

"We won't be able to afford camp if we pay for the surgery," my dad says. I figured on that, but since I'll have it done during the summer, sports are out anyway. The last thing you want is to be smacked in the face with a softball.

And that's it. Meeting over.

I go into my room, close the door, drop on the bed, and dance on my back with my arms and legs in the air like I'm Horace waiting for someone to scratch my stomach. Then I speed-dial Mel.

"Way to go, baby girl," she hoots. "You have to call my guy. You have, have, have to."

"I'm going to see a couple of people before I decide who." We talk more about how good she feels about the way she looks now.

"Keep the end result in mind," she says. "Don't get hung up on the surgery."

That reminds me of Mr. Wadler, last year's history teacher: "The end justifies the means."

Within days, I've set up two appointments. One is with Mel's doctor, and the other is someone recommended by a family friend who's a doctor. I won't tell anybody else yet, other than Mel and Katrina—not even Jen. I can't always trust her to keep things to herself. If rumors start circulating at school, everyone will start looking at my nose, if they didn't before.

THIRTY

To celebrate Katrina's upcoming surgery and my parents agreeing to mine, Mel, Katrina, and I get together again for lunch and shopping. We start at Henri Bendel where we sniff a bajillion fragrances, even though after four or five, your nose-brain connection flatlines.

But never mind, Mel is on a mission to discover something new and sexy, her "signature scent." Her latest obsession came from a magazine article about French women and their scent identities.

"The women's lovers could pick them out in the dark by the way they smelled," Mel says. "How hot is that?"

After exhaustive sampling, Mel finds something by L'Artisan Parfumeur. It has "notes" of tuberose, honeysuckle, and rare flowers, the saleswoman says.

"Rare flowers?" Mel raises an eyebrow. Her platinum card practically ejects itself from her wallet.

What do I buy?

Hold the front page: a black T-shirt. It costs twice as much as a Gap Favorite tee, but Mel swears it looks way better. She goes on about the European cut, which I don't really get, but I trust her on it. Katrina settles on a multipurpose lipstick, eye shadow, and blush stick in one, as if that's crucial because she's this high-powered executive who desperately has to streamline her life and lighten her Kelly bag, and anyway, it's so worth fifty dollars. She also buys a pink rhinestone collar for her favorite dog at the shelter.

"I know she won't realize it's special," she says, "but..."

"You're so sweet," I say.

Mel gives her a look.

All that took four hours and we need to refuel, so we go directly to Burger Heaven. This time the conversation is more about Katrina and me. At least at first. I tell Mel I'll be seeing her doctor first.

"Yes." Her fist shoots into the air.

"After that, I have an appointment with Dr. Kevin Miller who was recommended by a doctor friend of my dad's. He's head of the department at NYU Medical Center, and he spends two months each year in Africa doing reconstructive facial surgery on children."

None of that seems to matter to Mel. He rates a shrug from her, or maybe more aptly a one nose rating out of a possible five.

"Do you know how totally gorgeous the three of us are going

to look next time we get together?" Mel says. She reaches out to grab my hand and Katrina's as if we're about to start a séance. Katrina doesn't bother telling us the name of her doctor. He works in the local hospital, so there's no chance we'll know it. She's having her blood work done in two weeks and the surgery will be two weeks later.

Mel looks at her quizzically. "You nervous?"

Katrina shakes her head. "Just impatient."

"What about you, Al?"

"Yes and no…at least I'll be totally out."

"The hardest is the night before," Mel says, giving me a sidelong glance. "You're thinking about all this awful stuff, blah, blah, blah." She stops there. "My advice is hit the gym, run on the treadmill for an hour, lift weights, and totally destroy yourself the day before. Then when you get home, you'll fall dead asleep. You can't go to the gym for a month afterward anyway, so you might as well bust your tail while you can. You'll be up at the crack of dawn the next morning, so you won't have a chance to think about anything."

I'm relieved when she zooms into a discussion of school and John. It looks like Katrina feels the same way. When the check comes, Mel grabs it.

"On me," she says. We thank her and hug before we go our separate ways. Outside the restaurant, Mel walks over to a parked car that isn't hers. What is she doing? A moment later she squats down to look at herself in the side-view mirror.

✂---------

Amber calls me after school. It isn't about English. I know that right away. I'm guessing it's about her mom.

"Can you meet me at Starbucks now?"

Even though I was in the middle of writing an essay, I walk up to First Avenue and 75th Street. I spot a free table in the back, drape a scarf over it, and then get in line. Amber comes in a few minutes later.

"What are you getting?"

"Cinnamon Dolce Latte."

"Me too." As if she can't deal with deciding.

We make our way to the back, sidestepping a stuffed bear that was thrown to the floor by a pink-faced toddler who looks like she's about to explode. I can see why. It's about eighty degrees in Starbucks, and she's belted into her stroller in a padded snowsuit. Her mom is on her cell.

Amber studies me across the table. She's still wary, afraid to drop her guard.

"So what's up?"

She sighs. "Josh wants to take over my life, you know?"

How would I? I've never had a real boyfriend. "How do you mean?"

"He's all over me." She lifts a bag of sugar and shakes it so the contents land at the bottom. She tears it open and very, very slowly sprinkles the sugar into her drink, grain by grain by grain. "I don't want to be with him every minute of every day…" She lets her voice trail off, then she looks at me. "Do you ever get like short of breath?"

"No."

"He makes me nervous," she explains, "so I can't even catch my breath." She breathes in and out as if she's testing to see whether she still can.

"So stop seeing him."

"It's not that I don't like him…It's just…Well, my shrink says I have to think about me now. She says I don't have to cave in to the pressure."

I didn't know she was seeing a shrink, but it makes sense. "So tell him you're going through a lot. Say you need time to yourself." Probably the last thing on her mind is that if she ditched Josh, half the girls in school would follow him on their knees to take her place.

She lifts her cup, takes a small sip, and decisively puts the cup down. Then she reaches behind her neck and unfastens the clasp of a gold chain holding a heart-shaped locket. After a brief glance at the back of it, she tosses it into her handbag on the floor.

THIRTY-ONE

Speech. First period. Now that I've given my talk on baking a strawberry cake, I can breathe easy. I sit back and relax while the last four or five people sweat out their speeches before we move on to another unit. I'll be less anxious next time around, I'm sure.

I take out a pen and doodle as I wait for Jeffrey Stein, the next speaker, to start. But before he does, Mr. Scott holds up his hand and walks to the front of the class. He's excited and he's hoping it's contagious. I'm not sure that's a good thing. I hear the words, "next unit." In case I want to relax.

"So now you know you can communicate with an audience. You've stood up here, and you've done it. You're all accomplished speakers. We've heard about winning football games, the new family car, baking a cake, summer camp…" His voice trails off.

Before he was a teacher, Mr. Scott was an actor. Someone

said he had a part in a major Broadway show. Since he ended up teaching, I'm thinking he probably wasn't that big a deal as an actor. Maybe like most of them, he spent more time going to auditions than learning lines and being on stage in front of a real audience.

Now he's looking out at us—one by one—trying to make eye contact. There's a flirty look in his eyes, not that he does anything to me, but I see where he's going with this. He wants us to get on board.

Right then, I know for sure that what's ahead is going to be harder than baking a strawberry cake that doesn't fall. Or parading in front of the room in giant rollers.

"Our next unit," he says, "is about truth."

"Huh?" somebody in the back mutters. That sets off a round of snorts and snickering.

"Truth," he says again, giving it added weight and drama. "I want to hear speeches about who you are. What's inside you. Things that are uniquely important to you." A pause to let that sink in.

This is not happening.

"We're getting up close and personal. No more speeches about the car of your dreams. A trip to Vegas. Or your to-die-for designer clothes."

He doesn't mention Florence Singer's speech, the only serious one, about the first edition of *A Farewell to Arms* that she bought in a thrift shop for two dollars when it was worth five hundred.

"We're going to talk about joy, fear, sickness, loss, rebirth, love," Mr. Scott says. "Speeches from the heart."

David Craig makes a sound like he's croaking. Mr. Scott ignores it.

"I don't really understand what you mean," Florence says.

I love her at that moment.

"Okay," Mr. Scott says, welcoming a serious question from a serious student. "Tell me about the first time you fell in love."

Hel-lo...Florence?

"Or talk about how you felt when your grandma died." There's a pause. "I want to hear what was going on inside your head and your heart when you said good-bye to cousin Johnny, an only child, who joined the Marines and was sent overseas. How did you feel? Were you proud? Sick with fear? Afraid you'd never see him again? All of that? Were you so overcome that you couldn't be there the day he walked out of the house?" He pauses to let that sink in.

"Speeches from the heart," he says again. "I want you to reach inside yourselves. It won't be easy...but you can do it. We start in two weeks." His arm shoots out and points to David Craig. "You're first."

✂ - - - - - - - - - -

Amber comes over to me when we're in the hall and shakes her head back and forth slowly. "Shit, double shit. *What* am I *going* to do?"

"Read your diary. I don't know."

"I don't need this," she says, still shaking her head emphatically. "I really have enough going on now."

I feel just as out of joint. Public speaking is bad enough, but now we have to deal with putting what's in our head out there. Why? Why would you want to share your innermost thoughts with the losers in your class? What was I going to share—self-loathing? How on some days I want to hang dark scarves over the mirror in my room because I hate what it reflects back?

Josh walks by then and Amber turns slightly so they don't come face to face. He's not in our speech class, so at least she doesn't have to worry about him giving a talk about her. I glance at my watch.

"I'm late for math, but call me later. Maybe we can figure something out."

Amber hangs back to give Josh a chance to walk down the hall, but he walks backward, pointedly staring at her. She lifts her chin up and fixes her eyes straight ahead.

Maybe Amber's speech should be about avoiding the truth.

THIRTY-TWO

So Dr. Jordan is an orchid freak.

They're everywhere in his office. My mom leans over to me. "Maybe he operated on a grateful board member from the New York Botanical Garden," she whispers. We look at each and laugh softly.

The teachers have a study session so I'm off on a weekday— that's why they were able to squeeze us in. We check in at the front desk. The nurse who greets us has flawless skin and perfect features. I can't help wondering how much surgery she had and whether Dr. Jordan did it. She smiles back at me as though she knows that everyone wonders the same thing. I'm given forms to fill out, and we're told to sit in the waiting room.

At a round wooden table we pick up magazines. Mel was right. It's like a Library of Congress for fashion and design magazines. They must subscribe to every European magazine published. One cover has a picture of a bungalow up on stilts over the water with gauzy curtains surrounding a king-sized bed. Probably a honeymoon cottage in the South Pacific. It's the kind of place where I imagine that Dr. Jordan's patients go.

My mom and I sit together on a long, white silk couch with small purple needlepoint pillows with orchids on them. We arrive on time to the second because if we missed this appointment, we'd have to wait months for his next opening. I don't know if it helped me get an appointment sooner or not, but when I called, I told them I was a friend of Mel's.

Italian *Vogue* is in my lap, but I'm not reading it. I'm staring at the heavy, milk-white silk drapes hanging on the sides of the windows from thick brass poles. They're the kind with so much fabric you could completely disappear behind them if you were playing hide-and-seek.

I sneak a glance at the other two people waiting. One is older than me, maybe nineteen or twenty. Whatever she has that needs fixing is invisible to me. I doubt she already had the surgery because I've heard they don't put the before patients with the afters. The other patient waiting is a woman about forty. Alligator bag. Our eyes meet and mine drop back to the magazine.

Finally, another nurse who also looks like a model calls my name. We follow her into a room that's more like a medical office. No orchids here. I sit on the padded leather exam chair with a big lamp above it like the kind you see in dentists' offices. My mom sits to the side on a small, backless stool. The room is all white and immaculate. The lighting is bright. Other than a small mirror, a stainless steel container that looks like it holds cotton balls, and a prescription pad, there's nothing on the counter. I stare at a small black-and-white photo of the ocean, the only decoration.

A door opens slowly and Dr. Jordan walks in. I know it's him because I've seen his picture. He's about fifty. It's hard to tell if he had surgery. His face is smooth, but not that smooth. There are little crinkly lines on the sides of his eyes. He's slightly tan like he just came back from sailing. He smiles and sits in front of me.

"Hello," he says. He glances at my mom and then back to me, holding my eyes. He makes it clear he'll be talking to me, not her. I like him already.

"How can I help you?"

"I want to have my nose done."

He asks my age and only then looks down to read the chart. We talk about why I want it done, and when I decided. I point to the bump. I remember what Mel said about how he looked at her and asked her to turn left and then right. He takes his finger and presses it to one side of my nose and then the other. He rubs his finger along the bump as though he's measuring it. He asks me to look up and then down. Do I have breathing problems? Allergies? Then he looks inside my nose.

After just a few minutes, I hear, "I think you're a good candidate. We can smooth the bridge and overall just narrow it a bit." He looks at me intently as if he's trying to see whether I have any deeper issues that I haven't brought up.

"Questions?"

"When can you do it?"

He smiles. "My appointment secretary knows more about my schedule than I do. Any medical questions?"

So I'm a dimwit. "How long will it take?"

"Half an hour to an hour." I'm surprised. I thought he'd say two hours. We talk about recovery time, and how long I'll have to stay home before I can go out. "Anything else?"

I shake my head and he looks over at my mom. She asks whether it would be better to wait until I'm older in case my face grows.

"Once a girl is menstruating, there won't be any dramatic change in face size or proportions," he says. He pauses. "In terms of how she feels about herself, though…"—he looks at me—"that's her decision."

He likes to wait, he says, until girls are sixteen or seventeen. He says something about girls coming to terms with the psychological issues by then. Since I'll be sixteen at the end of the summer, and I'd have the surgery just before, he doesn't object.

A few polite seconds go by as if we're thinking about that. He gets up and says we can talk to the appointment secretary, if we're ready, or just think it over. He slips out the door before we answer.

"Businesslike," my mother says softly.

We'll be seeing another doctor before we decide anything, so we don't ask to talk to the secretary. As soon as we're out of the elevator and on the street, I call Mel.

"Didn't you totally love him?" she says.

THIRTY-THREE

Katrina calls the night before her surgery.

"How are you?" I'm starting to talk like Mel.

"Hmm…uh, nervous?"

"It'll go fine. You'll be gorgeous. No, actually you already are gorgeous. You'll just be more gorgeous and I will totally hate you." My nervous laugh, then silence. "What time are you scheduled for?"

"Seven…I know I'll be up all night."

"I'll be with you in mind and spirit, remember that."

"Thanks, Allie," she says. "I love you."

"Love you too, Katrina."

I didn't expect the conversation to be so strained. I'm nervous for her. I really do love her. I never had a sister, but if I did, I'd want someone just like her. I think of what she endured and how she goes on like it's something in her past that she can totally handle now.

"Anything new on your end?"

She wants to change the subject. I already told her about seeing Dr. Jordan.

"I'm seeing another doctor next week. After that, I'll just go with my gut. Until then, I'm going to hold off thinking about it."

Katrina's mom calls her for dinner.

"Gotta go," she says. "Steak and fries, my favorite meal."

The day before surgery, you're not allowed to eat anything after twelve at night. "Call me the second you get home."

"I swear."

"You swear you swear?"

"I swear."

I think of Mel's last words the night before her surgery: "It's all in the name of beauty."

I don't bring that up now.

THIRTY-FOUR

Katrina's in a hospital having surgery to change her face—but more than that, her life—and even though I'm mentally with her, my life goes on uneventfully. That doesn't seem to make sense, except when you think about living in a city of over eight million people. Every minute, while some people are having open-heart surgery and lying in beds with machines breathing for them, others are searching for the right shoes for a new outfit or having their nails done. So never mind what makes sense.

I meet David for mentoring and that's a distraction. Instead of the library or his house, we go for coffee. He takes that as some kind of victory.

He doesn't bring up my nose or stare at me through the camera, and I don't talk about his makeup or hair color.

Only today, he's not wearing any makeup.

You wouldn't think that eyeliner would have that big an

impact on the way someone acts. Except for David Craig. He's another person when he wears it.

David spots me as soon as he comes in. He nods as he walks to the counter. I already have my Caramel Macchiato and I'm sitting on a stool by the window so I can people watch. He comes back with his usual—house blend, black, grande. He sits next to me, making a point of looking at my cup. He sniffs.

"What?"

"Why don't you just order cake?"

"Because I don't want cake."

"Same calories and sugar," he mumbles.

I ignore him.

I flip open the book and slide it over to him. A lot of what we're learning overlaps with what we're doing in speech because it's about writing clearly and succinctly. That gets me back to thinking about personal truth. I turn to him. "What are you doing your speech on?"

He bites the corner of his nail. He's worried. A side of him I haven't seen before.

"Dunno. What about you?"

"I'm going to see what you do. You're first so you have a chance to shock people."

"Talk about how you feel in front of the camera," David says, deadpan. "Why you're uncomfortable."

"And you could talk about why you don't exist without your camera. Or why you wear makeup."

"Okay, I will," he says. "But then you have to talk about the way you feel about yourself."

Why should I take him up on it? I don't have to answer to him. I may not like myself, I may not be proud of what I see in the mirror, but there are other truths I could talk about.

"You're first. How do you know I'll live up to my part of the bargain?"

He snaps my picture. "I don't."

THIRTY-FIVE

In some way, I do get David's obsession with his camera because ever since I was four, I've been fascinated with old family pictures and the stories behind them. My grandma had a brown leather album. She kept it in her top bureau drawer, and whenever we visited, I'd take it out and go through it. It had thick, tan paper pages that were so dry that the edges sometimes snapped off when you turned the pages. Each of the six photographs on each page was held in place by four tiny paper corners that were glued on.

None of the pictures were marked, though, so I didn't know who I was looking at. But one day I was staying over at my grandma's house while my parents were away, and the two of us looked at the book together. She told me who was in each picture and I wrote the names on the backs. I was always careful with the book. It felt like each picture was part of a person and their living, breathing soul was in my hands.

After my grandma died, my mom and I went to her apartment to pack up her things. We sat on the edge of her bed looking at the album.

"It's a good thing you wrote down the names," my mom said, her eyes moist. "Otherwise now we'd have no way to find out who all these relatives are."

I felt sorrier for my mom than for myself. She'd lost her protector, her human security blanket. We hugged for a few seconds without moving, then got up without a word and started wrapping the album in tissue paper to take home and put in a safe place. Except for me and my dad, my mom has no other family now, just pictures and memories.

As soon as I come home from mentoring David, I go and look at the book. I'm curious about the family nose and where it came from. Besides my mom, who else looked like me? Who had the bump? Will the pictures offer hints of how my relatives felt about their noses? Did people in those days even think of things like that? Maybe all I'll see is whether they look shy or embarrassed to be in front of the camera. Most of the pictures, it turns out, were taken from too far off for me to see how anyone looked in profile.

But there is a picture of my mom. It must have been taken by my dad one day when they were at the beach. Her hair is slicked back and she's wearing a two-piece bathing suit. Nothing as tiny and revealing as kids my age would wear, but a bra top and boy shorts—enough to show she had a good figure. She's holding a beach ball up in the air like she's posing for an old-fashioned ad and she thinks the idea of the picture is a joke.

What stands out most is that she looks happy, completely happy. Her face is glowing, and it gives her a whole deeper level of attraction. I never really thought of my mom as beautiful, but in this picture she is. She's a perfect model. She radiates beauty. I take the picture and go looking for her. She's sitting in the living room reading the newspaper. I hold it out to her and she smiles.

"Question...I don't mean this as insulting or anything, really, but..." I pause.

"What?"

"Were you ever self-conscious about your nose? I mean the bump...you know...because in this picture, I can't imagine that you ever felt what I do."

She looks at me and pauses. "I don't think I was ever as hard on myself as you are," she says. She looks off like she's trying to remember her life at sixteen. "Maybe it was just the time. We didn't look at models in Victoria Secret catalogs, things like that...And when I was growing up, surgery wasn't an option for me or anyone I knew—our families didn't have the money. But sure...I was aware of my nose." She looks out the window and then back at the picture.

"There are some things in life you get past," she says in a slow way that sounds like she means it will take twenty years more of life to do that. "Then later on when I met your dad, no, I didn't think about it." She smiles. "He just made me feel beautiful...We were soul mates and I was happy." She shrugs.

"That was all." She looks off into the distance. "Good relationships nurture you. They help you find yourself and who you are. I don't mean just relationships with boys or men. Relationships with your family, with your teachers, your friends, even people at your job. They shape you," she says. "You're young, so you'll see…It takes time."

She narrows her eyes questioningly. "Does that help?"

Yes and no. I'm not my mom. She's different than I am. She grew up at a time when kids my age didn't have their noses fixed, at least not that often. You lived with things because you had no choice. But now we do have the money and get our noses fixed. It's not that big a deal.

"You're different." I leave it at that.

I'm the one who's unhappy, not her. Should I hold off for ten years? That's an eternity. Everything in my parents' lives is wait and see.

THIRTY-SIX

I put the album away and focus on Katrina. While I was eating breakfast, I was in the OR with her, then the recovery room. By the end of the day, I half expect to look in the mirror and see a new nose too. Maybe that should be my speech. How Katrina's surgery changed me.

By dinnertime, I'm not seeing the humorous side of it, though. She should have called.

Mel answers on ring one. "This is exactly what we went through with you."

"She's probably feeling crappy, and that's why she hasn't called."

"She promised."

"So did I," Mel says. "But I fell asleep when I got home, and when I woke up, my whole face ached. It felt like someone had packed my head with cotton."

"Let's wait until tomorrow," she says. "Then we can try her again."

My mom, who sees me in the kitchen staring into space, senses I'm crazed and gives me a concerned look. That's all it takes for me to tell her.

"There are always delays," she says. "Her doctor might have been late."

She's a world-class worrier, but right now she doesn't look particularly alarmed, which helps.

After dinner, I go online. I talk to Jen, Katie, even Photo-Op, David's screen name. He says he accepted my challenge.

"Okaaaaaay."

Only I can't focus on David right now. All I know is that I haven't heard from Katrina. I call her house at nine because I can't wait for tomorrow. Five rings and then the recording. When I hear, "In an emergency, I can be reached on my cell…" I scribble down her mom's cell number.

If they're stuck at the hospital, does her mom want me bothering her? She doesn't know me. We've never met. She's a nurse with a full-time job, and on top of that, she has to take care of Katrina. It's already late, and they woke up at five. I'll take Mel's advice and not try her again until morning.

I get into bed and turn on the TV, then pick up a new book I just got. I'm about to open the cover when I hear an incoming text. I glance over at my phone on the nightstand.

It's from Mel.

Al, it says. There's a problem.

THIRTY-SEVEN

"What happened?" I'm yelling into the phone at Mel.

"I don't have the whole story yet," she says as seriously as I've ever heard her. "But a friend of Katrina's mom answered her cell for her." She takes a deep breath. "The surgery part went okay." She stops. "But Katrina must have had some kind of bad reaction because after she came to, she started crying and screaming like she was going crazy."

"From the anesthesia? Does that happen?"

"I don't know," Mel says. "I don't think it happens a lot..."

"But she's okay now, right?"

"I don't know. The hospital turned off her phone."

"I remember how you sounded after the surgery. You said you were glad it was over."

"I had the sponges in my nose," Mel said. "I couldn't breathe and my throat was dry, but I wasn't upset. I didn't cry or anything."

"It sounds so different with Katrina."

"They said she was sobbing," Mel says. "And the more she cried, the harder it got. They called her doctor in and he had to give her something to calm her down. They want to keep her there for observation."

"Oh God." I can't say anything to Mel. She doesn't know. "What did the doctor say?"

"I don't know," she says. "I'm freaked."

"Mel," I say finally.

She takes in a breath and lets it out. "What?"

"You don't know what really happened, do you?"

"What happened when?" she says.

"When she broke her nose."

"The car accident?"

"There was no car accident. It wasn't like that."

"What do you mean?"

"She made that up to explain what happened to her nose," I say.

It freaks Mel out to hear this.

"I didn't know she had secrets from me," Mel says.

"Her dad did it," I whisper.

I've heard about post-traumatic stress disorder. When she was unconscious, maybe everything haunting her got larger in her mind, like a bad dream that stays with you and upsets you even after you wake up. I go online. Sometimes when teenagers have anesthesia, it says, they wake up crying because the anesthesia seems to put them in touch with their inner thoughts and conflicts. You suffer from stress for a long time after something bad happened because your mind won't let you forget.

It's clear to me now why she went into hysterics. You can't keep all that inside and pretend it's not there.

It's like swallowing poison and trying to live.

THIRTY-EIGHT

I get to speech early. School seems like a safe haven. David Craig is in his seat already. He's psyched; his face gives him away. Something about his eyes, the way they shine as if he's electrified inside. I feel the way he did when he looked at me through his camera lens and saw something I didn't know he could see. Cameras don't lie, and neither do faces, if you look hard enough.

We're allowed to have notes, but he doesn't. Did he memorize it? Will he be spontaneous? That's dangerous. With a sea of eyes staring at you, things don't always go as smoothly as you imagine.

We usually hear one or two speeches each class. Then we judge. Pros? Cons? Mr. Scott has driven the point home several times that he wants constructive criticism, not personal attacks.

What you can say:

I couldn't hear.

The argument wasn't made persuasively.

The speech lacked organization.

What you can't say:

It sucked.

I was totally bored.

Sometimes Mr. Scott videotapes us so we can evaluate ourselves. I don't know about anyone else, but I can't stand to see myself. There it is, up close and impossible to deny. The profile. The way I look when I talk and smile.

The bell rings and everyone is seated. Only Mr. Scott isn't in class. Is he absent or just late? Minutes go by. It's now seven after. David's watching the door. I want him to turn around so I can offer a look that says, "I know how you feel." He got stuck being first. What he does will influence everyone else.

Will he open up? Take risks? Or just go with safe and maybe dull?

At ten after the hour, the class goes from quiet to noisy. People in the back are talking. Then they're out of their seats. Somebody flies a paper airplane across the room. Somebody else takes out a cell and makes a call, ignoring the school rule that if you're caught talking in the building during school hours, your phone is immediately confiscated.

I watch David. None of what's going on seems to affect him, if he's taking it in at all. He sits there totally self-absorbed.

Then Mr. Scott rushes through the door. It takes everyone a few minutes to dart back to their seats and settle down. Cell phones vanish. He drops his briefcase near his desk with a thud, apologizing hurriedly for being late—something about a student in another class needing help. He gets points for not lecturing us on being out of control. He wastes no time looking out at the class as he peels off his jacket and lifts his chin toward David.

"Ready?"

David barely nods.

Mr. Scott points a finger at him. "You're on." He steps away from the desk, carrying his chair to the side of the room. He turns it around and straddles it, pushing up the sleeves of his red V-necked sweater before crossing his arms over the seat back.

David walks to the front of the room, a stone-cold-sober expression on his face. Head-to-toe black. Hair, eyes, turtleneck, jeans, sneakers, socks. The tip of the camera sticks out of his jeans pocket. He looks out at the class, briefly making eye contact with us, one by one.

"We're talking about truth," he says. He shoves his hands into his back pockets and leans against Mr. Scott's desk. A second later, *Boom!* An explosion like a gunshot reverberates throughout the room. Everyone bolts upright in their seats.

"What the hell was that?" someone yells from the back.

"Terrorist attack," someone mutters, and then laughs. "Take cover."

Then we see. The ceramic mug on Mr. Scott's desk smashed to the floor, sending pens and pencils up into the air like buckshot. If anyone was asleep, they're not anymore. Everyone bursts out laughing with nervous relief. David immediately leans over and starts to scoop up the pens. If he's embarrassed, his impassive face gives no hint. Mr. Scott shakes his head definitively.

"Leave it," he commands. "Forget it. Go on." He throws a menacing glance out to the class, which immediately halts the laughter.

David waits a few seconds, staring at the floor as if to get back into character. I feel for him; I can't help it. He sneaks in a breath. "So if we're talking about truth, I'm going to tell you why I live behind my camera—and wear makeup."

He glances at me quickly, then pauses and pats his pocket.

He's really doing it. I lean forward in my seat. I didn't expect it. Part of me is invested in this.

"My younger brother is...uh...not like me or most other kids," David says. He pauses to let that sink in. His eyes meet mine briefly again, and then he looks away. "And it has nothing to do with the fact that he plays basketball and I don't. Or that he's an A student and I'm...not. Or that we listen to different music. Or that I'm into photography, and he doesn't even know how to hold a camera." He smiles a half smile, stares at the floor, then looks up.

"What it has to do with is biology. And destiny." He pauses. "When he was twelve years old, he found out he had a problem. Something that it's hard to stand up here and talk about to the whole class." He shifts uncomfortably, looking at the back of the room.

"At first I didn't think I could do it." He rubs the side of his face. "Then the more I thought about it, the more I realized that truth has power. And it frees you. Keeping it locked inside you doesn't do you any good. In fact, it makes you crazy. The only thing to do with that weight is to share it. So I'm going to tell you about my brother and how his problem changed me and my life."

I saw David's brother for just a few minutes at his house when we were in the kitchen studying. He was tall like David, with shy eyes, shaggy brown hair, and a warm smile. We didn't exchange a word, but I remember thinking he looked vulnerable, approachable, the kind of person you could imagine having for a friend. I don't know why I felt that way. I guess it's something you just sense when you see someone for the first time. I turn my attention back to what David is saying.

"Three years ago, my brother went to the doctor for tests because he got sick with something he thought was the flu." He crosses his arms over his chest. "We waited almost two weeks to hear. We were sure that by the time the results came back he'd be better, on his feet, and the tests would turn out to be a waste of time.

"Only he didn't get better.

"And finally, the doctor called.

"For a few minutes," he says with an anxious laugh, "we thought he was confusing my brother with someone else. Doctors make mistakes all the time. Every day there's a story about a doctor who screws up and get sued. Everyone knows they're not always right.

"But it turned out that this doctor wasn't confusing my brother with anyone else, and no one in the family could believe what we heard. So my parents took him to another doctor to have the tests repeated. Tests aren't always right. Labs screw up too. It might have all turned out to be a big mistake. It could easily have gone that way.

"Only it didn't.

"Those tests came out the same way."

He takes in a labored breath, not hiding it now. It looks like he needs extra air to go on. David doesn't name the disease, but I hear chemo and know. "After about a month, the drugs to help him made him lose all his hair, even his eyelashes and eyebrows," David says.

"It's hard to imagine how different you look without your hair and your eyelashes and your eyebrows. How your face is robbed of so much character." He pauses and shakes his head.

"He turned into a ghost of himself," David says. "Kids in school made fun of him, and on the street, strangers would stare. He pretended he didn't care, but when we got home I'd hear him go into the bathroom and turn on the water hard. He thought it covered up the sound of him crying." David walks across the room toward the window, and then turns back to us.

"You can't know that and just throw up your hands. Only what can you do? I had to stop people from staring at him like he was some kind of freak. Baseball caps didn't help. Neither did bandanas. You could still see he was bald and his eyes looked sunken. One day, though, I watched a goth music video and something clicked about the makeup and what the guys did to really transform themselves. I started dressing like a freak. I dyed my hair—red sometimes, even vomit green."

Soft laughter.

"I put on black nail polish and eye makeup—every day. Everybody thought it was because I loved Billy Joe Armstrong. Well, I do," he says. He smiles. "And I kinda got into the look." Then the smile fades. He shakes his head back and forth. "But that wasn't why I did it.

"After that, people started looking at me more than him. Sometimes both of us wore makeup so people thought that we were both strange." He focuses on the back of the room as if he's deep in thought. Then he lowers his eyes to the class.

"That was two years ago," he says, leaning up against the side of the desk with his feet crossed at the ankles and his hands stuffed into his pockets. "Now...we think he beat it." He purses his lips together and nods his head. He reaches behind him and slides what looks like a piece of paper out of a large yellow envelope.

"This is Jesse now," he says, his voice catching. He holds up a photograph that looks like a neatly posed school picture. "All his hair has grown back and he looks like himself again. He looks 'normal,'" David says, holding up his fingers to make

quotation marks. And, 'healthy.' His doctors say his chances…
are very good.

"And every day, I pray that *this* time…they're right."

David walks back to his seat, and the next thing I know my
hands start to clap. Amber joins me, and little by little, so does
the rest of the class. When the applause stops, Mr. Scott walks
to the front of the room. He stands behind his desk and looks at
David. His face softens and he presses his hand over his heart.

Like the fastest draw in the West, David snaps his picture.

THIRTY-NINE

Florence is out sick with fever, so Amber's bumped up to number two on the sched. I can't help feeling sorry for her. It's the night before and she still hasn't written a speech. If it isn't bad enough that she's second, she's following David who has now raised the bar.

"I can't do it," she insists, raking her fingers through her hair. She does that when she's nervous. We're sitting on the floor of my room. We finished going over English, and now we're staring at random music videos.

"Of course you can." I try to sound convincing. "It doesn't have to be long. Ten stupid minutes."

"What should I say?" she hisses. "That my mom tried to kill herself? That I have a totally screwed-up life—or actually no life?"

I shrink back. "No," I say softly. "Maybe you can just talk about how hard it is when a parent is sick."

"Yeah? Sick with what? Tell them what she has so she comes off like a complete psycho? Tell them that they're talking about giving her electroshock treatments?" Her eyes fill with tears. "Please."

"I…I didn't know…"

"Yeah," she says, her head bobbing. She turns away and starts chewing at the corner of her nail, then abruptly stops. She's about to cry.

"Well…okay…" I need to step in and fill the void with something, not just sit there filled with pity. "What about something that happened to you? When I was little, I almost drowned at the beach. Has anything like that ever happened? You could just make a bigger deal of it than it was."

She's thinking about that.

"Something small even, like you lost a special locket that your grandma gave you or whatever. You don't have to tell them what's going on in your life."

"Small? I can't think of anything small to tell thirty-five dorks in the class." The stoic, default face is back.

"It's school. Just be honest about something, anything."

"My cat died when I was little," she offers up.

"Did you kill him?"

"No!" She's horrified.

"So say you did."

"Are you serious?"

I smirk and we both start laughing. "It's more how you tell it than what you actually say."

"I...I can't do that," Amber says dismissively. "I can't get up and talk in front of a class." She pushes her hair back off her face. "You're different," she says. "You're lucky."

"Why?"

"You have the head for school—you think on your feet. I don't. I zone."

"And you're lucky. You have the face of a model. You don't have to agonize about the way you look. You don't need rhinoplasty." I spit out the word like a curse.

She has a shocked look on her face. "No, but my whole life is a mess. People don't understand that."

"Look, you have to give a speech so why don't you do something about modeling—how it feels to get a job—or not get one. That's personal."

She narrows her eyes and shrugs. "Yeah, maybe," she says, packing up her bag. "It's getting late. I have to go."

✂-----------

I'm spouting advice, but have I written my own speech? Talk about how you feel in front of a camera and how you feel about yourself, David said. I never promised I would. What do I owe him, anyway?

Facing Surgery, by Allie Johnston. *You can't imagine how completely crazed I get when someone wants to take my picture. Why? I hate my nose. In fact it's so bad that I'm planning on going under the knife.*

Only I can't stand up in front of the class and say that because it's too awful to think of myself standing naked in front of the class as if I'm in confession or something. I mean, why would I do that? Because it's a stupid assignment and I'm desperate for an A?

I think about Katrina, which makes me wonder what's inside me that I haven't gotten to the bottom of. Would my head explode when I woke up from anesthesia? Would all my anger and self-hatred come out like an unstoppable flood?

FORTY

"It's the whole idea of being so helpless." I sip my black coffee.

David stares into his coffee cup.

"So victimized," I add.

No reaction. I shake my head. "Do you know what I mean?" Has he zoned or what? Finally he looks into my eyes.

"Sex abuse is like a cancer," he says. "It kills a lot of what's normal and healthy in you. And if you don't do something about it, it takes over your mind, killing your sanity."

"I never thought of it like that. You're right."

David doesn't know Katrina, so I think it's okay to tell him about her. Anyway, I'm not using her name. She's the one who went through it, but I need to talk about it so it doesn't take over my life—because what happened to her scares me. It's something I never imagined could happen.

I'm not tutoring David anymore. His grades are better now. It may have had something to do with how his head changed after his speech. Talking about truth helped him face up to things better, especially school.

His words changed me. I know that for sure.

"What do I do? What do I tell her?"

"Visit her. Be her friend," he says, holding my eyes. "But don't think you can make her pain go away."

So I go.

Mel and her mom pick me up, and we drive to New Jersey to see Katrina. My parents will do the reverse trip. Katrina's out of the hospital now, but she's staying close to home.

When we talked on the phone over a week ago, I told Katrina that I told Mel. I was afraid she'd be mad, but she wasn't. She says she's at the point now where she doesn't care if the whole world knows because she's relieved that she doesn't have to keep it a secret anymore. It's been almost two weeks since her surgery. We've both spoken to her on the phone. Before our visit, she texted: I'm better.

From the surgery or from what it did to her head? I don't ask. I feel some of the anxiousness I had before I saw Mel, only this time it's more complicated.

Katrina lives in a woodsy town that looks like it belongs more in Minnesota than in New Jersey. She has a two-story house with white siding and black shutters. Outside the glossy black door, a mat that says *Welcome*. We ring the bell and wait. Mel and I look at each other. "It'll be fine," she says softly. She's trying to reassure herself too.

A woman opens the door. She's tall like Katrina, so it must be her mom. But she's heavier, almost stocky. Her face is lined, her eyes puffy, her hair part brown, part blond, pinned up. It looks like she used to color it. Her face softens.

"Come in," she says. A moment later, a white Lab—a bleached version of David's dog, Horace—races to the door, her pink rhinestone collar glittering in the light. I kneel in front of her, and she starts licking my face.

"Her name is Faith. We were fostering her," Katrina's mom says, "but we couldn't let her go."

We follow her into a simple beige living room with brown fabric couches and a blond coffee table. There are some small leaf prints on the wall. Katrina's house is at the other end of the design spectrum from Mel's. It's like no one bothered after they found basic stuff to fill it.

Mel and I turn when we hear footsteps on the staircase behind us. Katrina walks toward us. Her hair and skin are even paler than I remember. She covers her face with her hands so that only her clear blue eyes show, and then she opens them as if she's playing peekaboo.

"What do you think?" she says shyly.

My mouth opens. My eyes start to sting. "You are sooo beautiful."

Mel presses her hands over her mouth and shakes her head in disbelief. "Omigod."

The three of us hug, and relief mixes with anxiety and uncertainty and comes out as a flood of tears. Katrina's mom smiles, then walks out of the room.

What shocks me is how the surgery has changed Katrina. Her nose is straight, delicate. She's like a flower that has come into bloom. Her nose matches her face perfectly. This is so different from when I saw Mel. Katrina isn't wearing makeup and her hair is loose, the way she always wears it. So the change is all from the surgery. I step back.

"How do you feel?"

She shakes her head and looks at us, then past us. "It was hard. I never expected my mind to take over like that." She shakes her head. "I...I...just don't know what really happened." Faith goes up to her and sits at her feet. Katrina kneels down and strokes the dog's back.

"You kept it inside for so long," Mel says, like to her it's obvious. "But now you're healing."

"Healing," Katrina says, with a sarcastic edge to her voice that I've never heard before. "That's everyone's favorite word these days."

I see a flash of anger in her eyes for the first time. It scares me to think of how much more must be inside her. I'm afraid to say something wrong, so I let her talk. She goes to therapy after school, she says. And she's in a support group for kids who've gone through what she has.

"It's so strange to talk about it," she says in her interior voice, the one with the secrets. "When it happens, you think you're the only one in the whole world it ever happened to. But then when it's in the open, you realize it happens to people everywhere, all the time."

She doesn't seem to be waiting for us to react, so we just listen. It comes as a relief when Mel breaks an aching silence and pipes up with, "I don't know about you two, but I am totally starving."

I want to hug her for that. We follow Katrina to the kitchen and take charge of making our own lunch, forming an assembly line making tuna salad sandwiches. Faith stands nearby, watching for crumbs. Katrina takes a few chunks of tuna and puts them in Faith's food bowl.

What's ordinary suddenly feels so reassuring. There's a radio on the counter and Mel puts it on. She turns the dial until she finds an oldies station. Music warms the room like good cheer.

"Baby, baby, baby, where did our love go?" Mel sings along with the Supremes, changing our shared mood from somber to upbeat. As Mel mashes the tuna, she dances in place and it makes all of us laugh.

"The tuna mash," she sings, like it's "The Monster Mash."

Nobody cares that it's cold out; we want to eat outside. We get our coats and put our sandwiches on a tray. Katrina doesn't stop to look at herself in the mirror in the living room as she passes it. It's like her head knows that her face is different now. She doesn't need to keep seeing the proof.

There's a blinding brightness in the backyard from the pale afternoon sun. It makes the dusting of snow on the ground glisten. We're surrounded by tall trees that look as old as time, their thick, knotty branches opening out like protective arms. Only now the tree limbs look silver-plated with glimmering ice. We each grab a sandwich, squeeze onto a swinging wooden bench, and push off with our feet. Mel takes out her camera and holds it out in front of us.

I can't help thinking that the number of bad noses has been whittled down from three to two to one.

The shutter snaps and Mel looks at the picture. "You moved the swing, dorks," she says. "It looks like there's Vaseline on the lens. Let me take another one." She counts again and we pose. Then we forget about posing as she keeps shooting.

In some strange way, living Mel and Katrina's lives along with them, at least for a while, has made me feel stronger and more at peace with who I am. I'm not sure why. Did giving them moral support make me stronger? Was it going through their surgeries vicariously?

This feels crazy and new.

Right now I'm like two people, the me that's in the moment and the me that's the videographer, recording me with my two best friends snuggling together. We're the same age, in the same grade.

But in our heads?
Who would guess how different we are.

FORTY-ONE

Back in school. I get to speech early. It's Amber's turn. Can she talk for ten solid minutes about truth and be convincing? Can she stand in front of the class and tell a moving story? I've never heard her say more than a couple of sentences at a time, maybe because she's hesitant about putting her thoughts into words. Still, maybe she can pull it off.

David walks in and sits at his desk. He faces forward, staring at the blackboard. He's reliving his speech. I see it. Other kids come in and glance over at him, but he's oblivious, a detached look on his face. Three more minutes until the bell.

Does Amber hope to make a grand entrance? The seconds tick by. Mr. Scott erases the blackboard, sending motes of chalk dust drifting through the air. Blank slate, the perfect backdrop for a speech about truth.

The bell rings. Mr. Scott closes the door and turns to the class, searching the room. "Anyone know where Amber is?"

Heads shake. "Paris?" someone calls out. Someone else laughs. Mr. Scott ignores them. "Let's give her a few more minutes." He opens his book and looks through it. He reminds Sharon Stein that her speech is due tomorrow. Teddy Morris goes the following day. Then me. I'm fixated on the second hand on the big, white face of the clock in the front of the room. Nine. A sixty-second circle: 9:01, 9:02, 9:03, 9:04.

At 9:05, Mr. Scott lifts a door-stopper-sized book off his desk. I read the spine: *Great American Speeches*. He turns through the pages and finally stops, going off on a boring tangent about the importance of opening lines and the power of words to change us. Please, not the "Gettysburg Address."

This is definitely filler.

He talks about the beginning and the end of a speech as the "verbal bookends" that support the content inside. Since I ate a light breakfast, my mind is picturing two slices of bread on either side of some chicken salad. My stomach starts to growl.

This is not fun. Or enlightening. I start to write my name in puffy, cheese-doodle-style letters. I look back at Mr. Scott and hear something about grabbing the audience's attention immediately, the way a good newspaper reporter starts a news story with a "gripping lead." He goes on. And on. Finally, the bell rings.

So Amber's way of handling truth is to cop out and not tell it. I'm annoyed. And disappointed.

But really? I can't blame her.

FORTY-TWO

I call Amber's cell. It rings and rings, and then it bumps to voice mail. A few minutes later my cell rings.

"Hi," she says. "What are you doing?"

"Talking to you."

"No, I mean later."

"Trying to write my speech."

Another pause. "I couldn't deal."

"If you don't give a speech, you'll fail," I say.

"I'll talk to Scott."

All Amber has to do is sit in front of Mr. Scott with her emerald eyes on him, and all his professional objectivity will fly out the window, like with every male in the universe whose brain goes soft when he looks at a gorgeous girl.

She'll tell him about her mom. He'll feel sorry for her. He'll try to separate himself and assume his role as teacher. But he'll look at how beautiful she is. And wounded. She'll ask him to understand. End of story, she'll be off the hook. The funny thing is, the talk she'll give him to opt out will be the same kind she could have given in front of the class to earn an A.

"Maybe he'll let you hand in something in writing."

"I never thought of that," she says.

"Anyway, he likes you." I shouldn't have said that. It sounds like I'm saying, "Your grade average doesn't matter because you can coast on your looks."

All she says is, "Yeah, I know...What's your speech on?"

I should know, but I can't seem to use the words "speech" and "truth" in the same sentence. It's forty-eight hours away, and not only haven't I written it, I haven't dealt with it.

"I still don't know."

"Tell me about it," Amber says.

"I can't handle the signpost-on-the-front-lawn approach to what's in my head." What I'm thinking and feeling about something, anything, is nobody's damn business. Definitely not my speech class's business.

Anyway, I may have to talk about why I can't talk about truth, because I have no family drama to discuss. "No relatives going off into the service. Normal parents. No one indicted. No one in jail. Disgustingly ordinary doesn't make for drama."

"You'll think of something," she says. "You're an A student."

Only now the A student who's always on time with her homework, even early, is ducking the assignment.

FORTY-THREE

The next day after we have coffee, David asks if I want to come to his house. "I want to show you something."

"What?"

"You'll see."

I call my mom and she says it's okay. Then the lecture about leaving before it gets dark and avoiding Central Park as it gets later. Seven o'clock is the witching hour for her. "Okaaay," I answer with the phone pressed to my ear.

Horace is waiting by the door, only this time he must recognize me because he doesn't bark. His tail is swishing back and forth. David drops his backpack and kneels down to scratch Horace's stomach.

"Dues must be paid," he says. Horace acts like it's the highlight of his day.

After getting milk and cake for both of us from the kitchen,

David stands by the refrigerator, playing with the tiny magnetic letters on it. But after a minute or two, I don't see a word, or even a sentence. I'm tempted to whistle to remind him I'm there. Finally he turns to me. "Let's go upstairs."

I follow him up the narrow spiral staircase. David stops outside a room with a closed door. It's dark in the hall, almost gloomy. I can barely see his face. He stops and puts his hand on the doorknob, turning back to me.

"You're going to freak, okay?"

"What?"

"I said you're going to freak."

"Are you a total pig, or what?"

"No."

"Do you collect tarantulas? Or have an anaconda for a pet?"

What is he getting at?

He shakes his head.

"I'm not into twenty questions, okay? Just open it." He turns the knob and pushes the door in. He flips the light switch and voilà—a room.

There are bookshelves, an unmade bed, folded laundry sitting in a pile on top of it, and above the bed, a Star Wars poster. Is that supposed to shock me? There's a corkboard on one long wall on the left that's covered with scraps of paper, newspaper articles, ticket stubs, a class picture, Horace's picture, magazine covers, a picture of Billy Joe Armstrong, and all kinds of other things you keep, like a map of your world.

Then I turn my head to the right.

And yes, I freak.

Hanging from what look like clotheslines that run from one end of the wall to the other are clothespins. But they're not holding wet laundry. Hanging along the line are a series of photographs.

"What is this?"

"My photographs."

"Why?"

"So you can see how I see you. And…so you can see yourself."

I go a few steps closer and look at about thirty eight-by-ten photographs—all of me.

Just me.

Some of the pictures were taken in speech. Some in the corridor when I didn't know he was taking them. One of me at lunch. And the pictures he took when we were together. Some when we first worked together at the library. Others from Starbucks. They capture fleeting expressions, private, intimate moments. Indoors, out of doors, the wind taking my hair, my eyes tearing from the cold. Happiness, surprise, uncertainty, anxiety, fear, distaste, hesitation.

I think of an artichoke and the time you spend peeling away the hard, spiny outer leaves to get to the tender heart. Only I didn't ask him to search inside me. I didn't want him to. None of this is his business.

"This is surreal," I say, even though I'm not totally sure what that word means. If it means otherworldly, or just a step out of the real world to the beyond, then yes, this is totally surreal. I turn back to him.

"Do you do this a lot?"

"What?"

"Take pictures like these of people you know?"

"Not on a regular basis."

"What are you going to do with them?" What I don't say is, why am I the subject for this character study? Who asked you to do this? It feels like a violation.

"C'mere," he says. "Look at how you look here. You don't know you're being photographed, so you're like a different person." He points to another one. "See how relaxed you look here? Then look at this one when you know I'm taking your picture. You see the tension? How you freeze up? When you're relaxed, you morph into…"

I'm not listening to him.

"So we've established that I don't like being photographed," I say, talking over him. "Is that your big revelation?" I shake my head. "Maybe you're applying to a photography program and this is your entrance exam. The many faces of Allie Johnston. I'm the field work, the test study."

"No," he insists. "I'm not applying anywhere and it's not some big revelation. It's not like that. It's just that now you can see how you change in front of the camera—how who you are doesn't always come through because of how you think of yourself."

Almost as an aside he says, "That's what I love about cameras, the way they can see. The way they can show you things your own eyes miss."

"Why don't you do a character study of someone else? Like yourself. Or your dog."

David shakes his head. "I'm not making fun of you."

No matter how hard I inhale, I'm not getting enough oxygen, even though the world is filled with it. I flash back to what Amber said when we were in Starbucks before she broke up with Josh. *Do you ever get short of breath?* Now I understand it.

"I have to go."

I turn and run from his room, finding my way down the dark staircase. I have to get out of his house and go over this. I don't know if he did anything wrong, but it feels that way. Who asked him to do a stupid character study of me? It feels like through the eye of his camera, he's privy to information about me that I myself don't know. My face, my nose. How much time did David study me? This is sick, obsessive.

I trip on the last step and land hard on my knee. "Shit," I mutter, trying to fight back tears. I stand up and run for the door, my knee throbbing. Then I stop. My backpack. Where did I leave it? I spot it lying in the corner and hoist it over my shoulder. Horace, who was lying on his bed asleep moments ago, sits up alert.

"It's okay, Horace," I whisper, even though it's not.

"Allie, wait."

David starts down the stairs, but I run out, slamming the door behind me. I run past the bus stop without slowing down. It will take me forty minutes to walk across town through the park. The sky's already turning an ashy blue and the sharp wind rubs my face raw, but I don't care. I don't care about anything.

✂------------

Dinner is spaghetti with meat sauce. Something I never turn down.

"I don't feel like eating," I tell my mom. A headache, I come up with. Not really a stretch. She thinks it's PMS and doesn't push. I get into bed and pull up the covers, staring at the ceiling, hoping some part of my brain will snap to and tell me why I feel that what he did was so wrong. Okay, he took pictures of me. But it was more than that. It was where he took the whole thing. I felt like a novel in school that everyone was discussing, analyzing, and dissecting, like a dead frog that was sliced open and spread apart. I was David's goddamn study project.

I grab Cubby, my stuffed dog who's almost as old as I am, and use his soft back as a pillow. I inhale his familiar, cottony smell, rubbing my chin over his worn, velvety back, the loose spidery threads faithfully holding his sagging head to his body. I hear the door open slowly.

"You okay?" my mom asks hesitantly.

I pretend to be sleeping and she closes the door quietly. I lie back and rethink the afternoon. I'm unglued. Open-heart surgery. His pictures left me exposed, vulnerable. There are places you don't want other people to go, and his pictures crossed the line.

FORTY-FOUR

I welcome school the next day and the noise. All the people in the hall during class change become a buffer between me and David and where we are. He's now three feet behind me in the corridor. I sense him on a rare frequency, the way dogs pick up sounds that humans don't.

But he knows I'm not letting him know I know. He's probably studying his latest round of undercover pictures. Maybe he's even putting together a series on my butt so I can see for the first time the roundness of the curves and the state of my ass compared to others in the universe.

Just being honest doesn't give him the right to hold up this giant mirror to everyone else. That's what really annoys me. Who asked him to play God?

I walk into speech. Sharon Stein is shuffling through what looks like an entire pack of white index cards. She seems to be compulsively pulling at the rubber band that's holding her ponytail, trying to readjust it in some way. Amber walks in a few minutes later. Dressed to kill. High-heeled boots, short black skirt.

I know where she'll be after school.

The bell rings and Mr. Scott jumps up and shuts the door. He nods to Sharon, who gets to her feet and goes to the front of the room. She opens her mouth and I hear:

"Whe-whe-whe-when I was little, I used to stutter a lot."

I sit up straighter in my seat.

"It was the most embarrassing thing in the w-world," she says. "I didn't have play dates with other kids because they made fun of me."

She segues into talking about a speech therapist in school who felt sorry for her. "With her help, I was able to get a little better," she says, "but not before spending hours at home crying because I wasn't like other kids."

Her speech is unusual, and I learn something about her from it. She mentions that when she sang in a school play—and in general when she sings—the stuttering seems to vanish. And once when she read a script for a school play, no one could tell that she stuttered.

I feel for her. It must have been frustrating and awful, but she dealt with it in front of the class. It took courage. It rang true.

David's watching her closely. No sign whether he liked her speech. But Mr. Scott smiles at her and starts to applaud. Amber turns to me and raises an eyebrow. Well, it didn't exactly move me to tears, her face says. I glance at her and then a lightbulb goes on.

In a millisecond, I come up with the subject for my speech.

FORTY-FIVE

After school I check my email. What I'm expecting is garbage, but what I see first is a message from Photo-Op.

Subject: I have to explain.

Click. I open the message.

I know you're mad at me, but try to understand me and why I took the pictures.

People make fun of me. They call my camera my security blanket—even my brain in a box. I don't have a life, they say. I'm just this jerk who runs around school taking pictures of everything instead of living.

There's some truth to that.

Ever since I started going to photo exhibits, the relationship between me and the camera and what it taught me about seeing things became more important than anything else. Edward Steichen said:

"Photography records the gamut of feelings written on the human face, the beauty of the earth and skies that man has inherited, and the wealth and confusion man has created. It is a major force in explaining man to man...and that is the most complicated thing on earth."

For me the best pictures show you things the naked eye misses. You see things in pictures the eye doesn't focus on because everything around us is in constant motion. Pictures show us hidden relationships and hidden beauty. And that fascinates me.

Maybe you think I see myself as this self-important asshole. Or as this great photographer. Well, asshole, yeah, kind of. But no, I'm no great photographer, not now, maybe not ever. But I'd like to be. And that's why I take pictures of everything, all the time. And if you don't know by now, I'm fascinated with you and the way you look.

In a good way, Allie.

By showing you the pictures, I was just trying to show you some of the Allie I see. I'm sorry if you're mad. You shouldn't be. It was a compliment. Nothing less.

Don't be mad anymore.

Please?

I go to the freezer and take out a container of Rocky Road. My mom always opts for healthy, so she must have thought it was sorbet and bought it by mistake. It's sweet and creamy. When I finish every drop, I go back to the computer and reread his email.

My fingertips sit lightly on the keys, waiting. I lift them to examine my nails. I bite a ragged cuticle. I thought I was mostly invisible to boys, and then David comes along and x-rays me. How am I supposed to feel?

Don't be mad anymore, he said.

I'm not mad at him anymore; I'm mad at his pictures. A picture is worth a thousand words. That's the problem.

FORTY-SIX

Something else is on my radar screen today, my speech.

"What are you doing it on?" Jen asks me at lunch.

"Physiognomy."

She squeezes her eyes shut. "What is that?"

"It's this pseudo-science that basically says beauty equals goodness and morality, while the ugly freaks of the world are stupid, lazy, or immoral."

"I thought it had to be about something personal," she says, scrunching up her face.

I shrug. "I'm going to talk about how stereotypes and typecasting people according to their looks are unscientific, racist, and unfair."

She snickers. "Has anything changed?"

"We're still influenced by how people look, but I think that most people in this century know that not being gorgeous doesn't mean there's something wrong with you," I say.

"You should talk about yourself and your nose," Jen says.

Duh, in case I didn't think of it? Does she really think I would do that?

"I have to go," I say, turning away. "I want to get to speech early."

✂ - - - - - - - - - -

The bell rings and my heart kicks my chest. Mr. Scott nods in my direction. Very slowly, I make my way to the front of the class, my hand clutching my index cards. Talk slowly, the voice in my head says. I look out at the class. I swallow.

"This is a speech about beauty. Beauty the way the world sees it and how it can affect us on a personal level."

I give background on how the Greeks defined beauty and then talk about classical Greek art and about proportions: how the Greeks thought the nose should equal one third the size of the face, and how centuries later, everything and nothing have changed.

Are their eyes glazing over, or it my imagination?

I talk about Hitler and his nonsensical theories of a superior master race. "We're all a mix of ethnic backgrounds, and I see that as a strength, not something that would diminish us in any way or make us inferior.

"I hope our generation takes a more enlightened view and doesn't judge people by how they look. What's important is who we are on the inside."

I slip back to my seat.

Silence.

No applause, no nothing. Certainly no one is moved to tears. I see blank faces. Someone yawns. Someone else lifts his backpack and starts stuffing notebooks inside it.

A benign nod from Mr. Scott. He studies me for a painful few seconds, narrowing his eyes.

Amber turns to me. "Good," she says in a small voice.

✂ — — — — — — — —

On the way out of class, David tries to reach me. I walk faster, but he's determined. He pushes his way through the crowded corridor so he can catch up with me.

"Allie," he says, nearly out of breath. "Don't feel bad."

I turn to him. "What?"

"Don't feel bad. You did the best you could."

I'm waiting for him to go on about how I failed to live up to our agreement, but he takes the high road. Points for that. What he does say: "Truce?"

"Or consequences?"

"What?"

"It's the name of an old game show," I say. "It was called *Truth or Consequences*." His face breaks into a small smile. "Okaaaay. Wanna get coffee after school?"

I'm not sure how to answer, but I feel the corners of my mouth turn up. I can't help it. He takes that as a yes. Just as I'm heading down the other corridor to go to Spanish, I hear, "Allie?"

I look back at him.

Click.

✂-----------

David and I are side by side at Starbucks. Not talking. The usual line of ten people is waiting as if they're giving out free iPads.

"What?" David says, looking at me.

"What what?" I shoot him an exasperated look.

"You're obviously down—so what is it?" He uses two coffee stirrers as drumsticks.

I'm not going to bring up the pictures again. What would be the point? "The stupid speech," I blurt out louder than I intended. "I'm sure I got a C minus or a D." He doesn't say anything, which makes it worse. "I couldn't do it."

He shrugs. "It wasn't a total cop-out."

He obviously has no idea how I feel so I turn to him. "Charades," I say. "Who am I?"

I start shaking my head, darting my eyes everywhere, my tongue moving back and forth in my mouth, my fingers wiggling in all directions. I probably look possessed, but I don't care.

David starts to laugh. "You're an epileptic. I don't know."

I stop and shake my head. "I'm a Cuisinart," I say flatly. "That's me inside. Mixed up. Thoughts and emotions pureed."

"You're funny," he says, his expression softening. "It's hard to talk about yourself. You did the best you could."

"Uh nooo, actually I didn't." I think of his speech. *"Truth has power. And it frees you. Keeping it locked inside you doesn't do you any good."*

He leans toward me. "Can I tell you something?"

"What?" My hands grab my napkin and start folding it into tiny pressed pleats. He's studying my face. It makes me nervous. Ever since Amber changed my hair and put more makeup on me than I usually wear, I've been going to school like that. Is he going to weigh in on that now?

"Two things," he says, touching my arm. "For what they're worth."

I continue pleating.

"First, I think you're way too hard on yourself."

I start to protest, but he holds up a hand.

"And second"—he pauses—"I think you're cool looking...really."

I stop pleating.

So not what I expected. It throws me. I glance at him, then my eyes robotically look down into my coffee cup as if something fascinating there requires my complete attention. He takes my silence as permission to go on.

"I know you're self-conscious...but I think you look kind of exotic, interesting. You remind me of the girls in European magazines. They don't look like everybody else, and that makes them..."—he's reaching for a word and I wait—"distinctive."

My cheeks are fuchsia, I just know. I've never mastered the art of taking a compliment. Maybe because I haven't gotten many?

"Thanks, whatever. I mean, I appreciate it. It's just...I don't exactly know...You know...It's just—"

As I'm stammering, trying to piece together a few intelligible words, he leans toward me.

"Allie?"

"What?"

"Shut up," he says softly.

Then he kisses me lightly on the lips. And I do.

FORTY-SEVEN

Dr. Kevin Miller's office isn't on Park Avenue. It's in a white brick medical building at New York University Medical Center, close to Bellevue Hospital where the trauma center is known for treating gunshot wounds.

I don't see runway model receptionists, a back entrance for celebrities, or rare orchids. The only thing green and growing here is a snake plant that my mom says is also known as mother-in-law's tongue. The pink ribbon around this one's pot makes it look like it was left behind by a patient who didn't want to bring something like that home.

We wait until my name is called. *Forbes*, *Newsweek*, *Smithsonian*, and *Golf Digest* are on the coffee table. I play a game on my cell and then text Mel.

Waiting to see Dr. Miller. Minutes go by. She doesn't answer. Did she get it? Does she even care anymore? Something about her not answering depresses me. Now that her surgery is over, has she abandoned me?

The nurse eventually calls us. She wouldn't win any beauty contests. She doesn't look like she's had plastic surgery or that it would make much difference if she did. Strangely enough, that puts me at ease. This isn't Dr. Jordan's perfect bubble of beautiful blonds and white silk curtains. This office shouts "real world."

Dr. Miller comes in almost immediately. He's tall with broad shoulders and a mixture of blond and gray hair. He looks like he was on the basketball team or played football when he was in college. He must have been hot then because he's cute now in an old-guy way. He gives me a warm smile and glances down at the forms I filled out.

The consultation isn't very different from the one with Mel's doctor. After the "tell me why you're here," I go on about the bump and my profile. Dr. Miller narrows his eyes. He listens hard as though he wants to hear not only my words, but also the thoughts behind them. By now I know that where you are mentally is a big chunk of how a surgeon sees you. You're not just a nose on two legs. If you're immature or loony tunes, they don't want you.

The exam doesn't take much longer than Dr. Jordan's. Dr. Miller touches, looks, and asks about breathing, allergies, or other medical issues. If I go with him, the surgery will be in the hospital, not his private office, but I'll go home the same day.

When it's time for questions, I ask him if he has a book of before-and-after pictures. He shakes his head.

"Every patient is different," he says. "You shouldn't base your decision on how someone looked before and after because that won't have any bearing on how you'll look." He also doesn't like computers that show you before and after.

"It's a marketing technique," he says. "What you can do on a computer isn't always what you can do in real life." It's like offering a patient "an implied warranty," he says. "And I can't give you that."

He tells me to think about it and talk to my mom. He glances at her briefly. "If you have more questions, pick up the phone."

We walk out and I turn to my mom.

"When you have two doctors who are both supposed to be equally good, how do you decide which one to choose?"

"You pick the one you're more comfortable with. They're both respected and experienced, so you go with your gut."

Going with your gut, my family's mantra. Beyond all their research, my dad trusts his gut. My mom does too. I know there's some scientific basis to that. I've read about how you should trust your instincts, especially when it comes to danger and you get bad vibes about a person or a situation, and your gut tells you to get away.

By the time we get out of the cab at our apartment, I decide that Dr. Miller is more down to earth and someone I can relate to better. The day after I see him, I call his secretary and set up an appointment for the day after school ends in June. I make a chart and start counting the days. About an hour later, I finally get a text from Mel.

Cool!

Okaaay.

FORTY-EIGHT

For the past month, Amber's been staying with her older sister who has an apartment on Sutton Place, a quiet part of the city right on the East River. The apartment has a terrace overlooking the water, and she asks me to come over and hang out with her there. Even though I'm not Amber's mentor any more since her grades are up, five o'clock on Tuesdays has become a routine for us, so now we do homework together.

"If I lived here, I'd ask my parents to move my bed outside so I could watch the boats go by when I was falling asleep."

"It's no big deal," Amber says.

I don't think she takes time to look at the view.

"My sister works full time and goes out a lot, so she's hardly ever here," Amber says. "And I don't like to stay home alone."

It's been almost a week since she missed her speech. When

I ask her what happened with Mr. Scott, she rolls her eyes. "He was sympathetic, sort of," she says. "But I could tell by the way he was listening to me that he was judging what I was saying like I was giving a speech."

"What did he say?"

"He understood that I was going through a lot, and he didn't want to add to the pressure, so he said I could take more time. I thought that was it, but then he added that when I was ready and felt better, I had to give the speech."

So now I'm feeling guilty on two counts. First because even though I'm Amber's friend, I agree with him that she shouldn't get a pass. And second, because I underestimated Mr. Scott. Maybe not every male is a complete pushover in the face of drop-dead beauty. "What are you going to do it on?"

I expect her to hesitate and look annoyed. She's probably thinking of something anti-school or anti-family. How could she not?

But I'm wrong.

She pauses for a moment and then points at me. "I'm doing it on you."

"Excuse me?"

"You. How we became friends."

"What are you going to say?" I already had a full frontal attack from David, so I don't need another one.

She flashes an enigmatic smile. "You'll see."

✂ - - - - - - - - - -

During the next class, those of us who've given our speeches get back our grades. David: A plus. He doesn't tell me. I peer over his shoulder and see an A written in red felt-tip pen that's about equal to the size of the E on top of an eye chart, so even someone half blind could see it. Sharon Stein: A. I don't see her paper, but I overhear her telling someone.

And me? I stuff the paper into my notebook before anyone sees it. I was right, a crapola C plus. And he was being kind. It deserved an F. For the first time I can remember, I feel a sense of shame. I've never gotten less than a B plus in anything except math.

"Interesting topic and decent delivery," Mr. Scott's scribbled note says. "But points off because you fell far short of going beyond your comfort zone to tackle the subject more intimately."

"Show some balls" should have been his next line. By not talking about myself and babbling on like a moron about a laughable theory of pigeonholing people favored by idiots, I made it clear I was a complete and utter loser. The saddest thing is, I'd do the same speech again.

✂ - - - - - - - - - -

Florence Singer, the butt of everyone's jokes, is back in school. She's over the flu and she's hunched over her desk gnome-like, reviewing her note cards. She doesn't look nervous. Florence never looks nervous. She looks prepared. I have no doubt that if someone swiped the cards off her desk, if wouldn't matter. She'd give the same A speech.

What will her topic be? We all know she's a genius, but we don't know Florence the girl, the person, the human being. Everyone writes her off. The non-person with the Mensa IQ. But when you have to talk about truth, you have to open yourself up and show your heart. At least the real A students do.

Kirk Morrison plants himself in the last row of every classroom because he flatlines in school and cannot perform except on the football field. Although he was suspended from the team for half a season last year for cursing out the coach, he starts making farting noises when he sees Florence and then segues into slurping sounds, whispering, "suck me," in a low, pervy voice that Mr. Scott can't hear, but I imagine Florence can.

Amber turns and sneers at Kirk. "You are a totally disgusting pig." I want to hug her for that because she's the only one who can get away with dissing Kirk without retaliation. I dread the thought of what he'd shout from the roof if I ever confronted him. He stops momentarily and laughs. I look at his eyes and think of the vocab word "reptilian."

Mr. Scott motions for Florence to start. She stands up and walks to the front of the room. Despite the tangled hair that falls around her shoulders and looks unwashed, and the baggy skirt, there's a serenity around her. She may not be the person anyone wants to look like, but that's not the issue. She knows who she is, I see for the first time, and her view of herself has nothing to do with her looks.

"I'm sixteen," she starts. "Nobody thinks of you as an adult when you're in high school. Nobody imagines that you have the talent to do what someone ten or even twenty years older than you can do. But I don't believe in categorizing people," she says, "or discounting them. I believe everybody should be judged for who they are and what they can do, no matter how old they are, so I decided that even if I was just a teenager, I was going to write a novel, get an agent, and sell my book."

"Hey, Nora Roberts," someone calls out from the back. Someone else laughs. Mr. Scott stands up and the room grows silent.

Florence pretends not to hear. She talks about growing up in a family of writers. "My mom's written thirty novels," she says, "ranging from murder mysteries to love stories. Three of her books have been optioned for movies. And my dad writes biographies. "Lincoln, FDR…" She rattles off other names, some I haven't heard of. "So it's no surprise that I inherited the bug."

From the back of the room Kirk snorts. Mr. Scott gives him a threatening look that shuts him up.

"Anyway, the idea for my novel came from the world around us," she says. "It's a sci-fi book about good and evil, and an elite class of women who decide they want to live in a world without men, a world where there's no need for armies because no one's fighting, and everything's equally distributed so there are no rich and no poor, and no hatred between different people. Everything's tranquil with all of the men gone. The society begins to function on a higher order." She pauses. "Then," she says, "one of the men returns."

I look over at Mr. Scott. He's charmed. He's leaning forward in his seat with a half smile on his face.

"So that's the book I wrote," she says. She laughs lightly. "And you'll have to wait until it's published to find out what happens. Anyway, I wrote it and rewrote it about twenty times until I was happy with it. I sent it to an agent who handles best-selling authors. Two weeks later, she called and said she wanted to represent me.

"Ask any writer how often that happens." She shakes her head. "When I confessed how old I was, I immediately assumed she might rethink her offer, but just the opposite happened. She was delighted. She said I'd get more attention because I was only sixteen. She sent out my book, and a month later, a publisher offered me a contract.

"This is a speech about truth, so now I'm going to tell you how I feel." She flashes an enormous smile and I realize I've never seen her do that. Before today, her face never gave away anything about how she felt. She puts her hand in the middle of her chest. "Over the moon," she says. "Nothing in the whole world could have made me happier than getting that phone call. I was accepted. Validated."

This gets me thinking. What would give me validation?

Here's someone who everyone in school rates a total loser, but wake-up call, she has a life. She's only sixteen and her name will be on a book that maybe thousands and thousands of people will read. So the next thing I'm feeling is admiration. Admiration and envy of Florence Singer, which is a new one. I go back to listening to her.

"No matter what else happens to me, I'll always have that feeling to hold on to," Florence says. She's quiet for a moment and then she looks out at us.

"Things in your life don't always go the way you want them to. You don't always end up with the people you'd like to end up with. With the friends you'd like to have—or even any friends at all…so you have to find things that make you happy and feel fulfilled. You have to search inside your heart and find work you love.

"But above all else, you have to have confidence in yourself and tell yourself you can do whatever you set out to do. That means you have to love and respect yourself for who you are and your special talents because we all have talents and we're all special—just in different ways. Thank you."

Mr. Scott gets to his feet and applauds, and the whole class follows him. No one is making fun of Florence Singer now. I have a feeling that even though it probably wasn't her intention, a lot more people will want to be her friend now because of what she's accomplished. It also hits me that her speech transformed her. She wasn't dowdy Florence Singer anymore.

On the way out of the class, I go up to her. "Your speech was amazing. I was blown away. Do you want to have lunch together?"

Florence looks at me as if she's never seen me before. "I usually don't have lunch," she says. "I go to the library to work."

"Just this once?"

She shrugs and says, "Sure," and I follow her out.

FORTY-NINE

Florence is in line getting her lunch while I sit down at the table with Jen, who isn't in our speech class. "I'm saving a seat," I say.

"For?"

"Florence."

She shakes her head like she didn't hear me. "Who?"

"Florence. Florence Singer." I point to her in the cafeteria line.

"Really, why?"

"To talk to her."

"I heard she wrote a book."

I nod.

"What's it about?"

"A world without men. A world without fighting."

Jen laughs. "She's probably gay."

I spring to my feet and grab my tray. "What she is is totally talented. She wrote a book and got it published, okay? Are you aware of how hard that is? I don't see what being gay or not has to do with anything. I think she is talented. And she's smart enough not to waste lunch hours dissing other people." I take my lunch and pivot, heading to another table, but then I stop and turn back to her.

"Jen, get a life."

I walk across the cafeteria and sit down somewhere else, watching Florence pick up her tray as she leaves the cafeteria line. A moment later Kirk walks in her direction.

No. Please, please, no.

A second later, *Crash.* Florence's head jerks up, surprised. Spilled tomato sauce with twisted strands of spaghetti, like engorged leeches, cling to the front of her white blouse and pale blue skirt, a Rorschach pattern spelling disaster. Her plate is on the floor in front of her, the plastic cup rolling off somewhere as if it's looking for a place to hide. The expected round of applause comes a moment later from everyone in the cafeteria.

I grab a handful of napkins off a table and go running up to Florence. I help her wipe the food away. She shakes her head like she's more bewildered than upset. Amber comes running up to us to help too. Kirk sits at a nearby table with a satisfied smirk on his face.

For the first time I'm thrilled to see David on the spot like a paparazzo. He's clicking away. He recorded the whole thing—

Kirk smashing into Florence and then Kirk's smug face afterward. My heart is pounding. I want to take the filthy tray and smash it over Kirk's head, then rub his face in the spaghetti.

But I don't.

My anger rises up and then spirals, filling me with a sense of clarity and elation. I stroll over to Kirk and duck down, putting my face so close to his that I smell his breath. I make sucking noises, just like the ones he did. "You are so getting thrown off the football team, you loser," I whisper. "Suck that up and see if you like it."

Amber watches, enjoying my performance. I half expect her to moon him. For the first time, Kirk is silent. He turns pale. The possibility of being tossed from the team for good never occurred to him. I see that now. The coach is strict about how guys behave in school. They have a code of ethics, as he calls it. If enough of us complain about Kirk and the coach sees David's pictures, I'm sure we can get him thrown off the team, or at least suspended. Amber turns to me and hoists her fist triumphantly. "Yeeees."

"If all the men in the world were like Kirk," I say, "a world without them would get my vote."

Florence stares at all of us and shakes her head. Before she walks away, she says, "I knew this was a mistake. I should have had lunch in the library."

FIFTY

What is Amber going to say about me? I feel like she's a friend who's a newspaper reporter and one day she informs me that everything I told her in private will be printed on the front page—and there's nothing I can do about it. Will she talk about how I see myself? About my nose?

I trusted her. I told her things that I never imagined I could. Would she betray me in front of the entire class? Would she talk about the things that I couldn't come to terms with to avoid talking about her own problems? We've become friends, but still there's this whole interior part of Amber that I don't know.

So translation: I panic.

Amber walks into class good to go. Her left hand is wrapped around a pack of index cards. Her fingernails are perfectly polished, blush pink. She makes her way to her seat. No Chanel suit today. Slim black jeans, a pale pink turtleneck. Flat black boots. If clothes could speak, hers would say "nonthreatening."

Mr. Scott motions for her to go to the front of the room. She walks up, head high, and then looks out at the class. At the last second, she looks over at Mr. Scott imploringly.

"I'm not good at this."

He shakes his head and looks at her skeptically. I doubt that, his expression reads. She turns back to us. "Okay." It's a decisive *I can do this* okay. I lean forward, my heart slamming in my chest, more afraid to hear her speech than I was to give my own.

"I had a hard time this year because..."—her eyes dart out the window and then back to us—"my mom was sick." She shakes her head. "I was depressed about it. I didn't do my homework, or much of any work for school. So my English teacher decided I was one of a bunch of kids who needed tutoring." She looks at me and then looks away fast, like she's trying not to laugh.

"I hated the idea at first. I mean, I didn't want to go to school in the first place and then I had to spend extra time on it?" She shakes her head. "Also who wants to get help from someone in your own class? But I had no choice. No one asked me what I wanted. As the saying goes, 'Life has a way of surprising you.'

"And it did.

"Sooo, this is a speech about how I became friendly with someone who I never would have become friendly with if I didn't give up on school and on myself."

She tells the class she didn't show up the first time we were supposed to meet and then tried to lie her way out of it.

"She didn't tell on me, but she could have. Most kids would have. Then when I asked her why she didn't, she didn't lecture me. She just let it go. Maybe she accepted me or realized I had a lot going on or whatever, but after that I figured if there was anybody I could learn from in my grade…" She shrugs and her voice trails off.

Is my face giving me away? I can't believe she's so up-front.

"I wanted to be like her," Amber says. "I wanted to be smart and confident and good in school and proud of what I could accomplish, not just somebody who everyone thinks is an airhead because all she's good at is posing in front of a camera. Really," she says, "I wanted to be able to hold my head up too."

She thinks I'm confident?

She pauses and glances at me, then looks away. "Anyway, they say that life doesn't give you more than you can handle. And that when you're ready to learn, a teacher appears. I found out I could handle my life, even if my mom was sick and I didn't know if she would ever even get better. But the truth is, I don't know if I could have gotten to that point if I hadn't met her because she's not just a good mentor, she's also a good listener."

She glances at Mr. Scott. "I might not be great at speech, but I learned that even when you think life is testing you by giving you more than you think you can handle, sometimes it also gives you ways to help you deal. Thank you."

She rushes back to her seat. I punch her in the arm and her face flushes with embarrassment. She tries to hold back a smile. A moment later she reaches over to me and slips something into my closed hand. I uncurl my fingers and see one of the silver rings she wears. I look at her questioningly. She takes a pencil and reaches over to my desk. On a sheet of paper sticking out of my notebook she writes, "Friendship ring, okay?" I nod.

As I'm about to slip it on my finger, Harry Thomas, the Olympian nose-picker who sits on the other side of Amber, leans over to her.

"Hey, Amber," he whispers. "Was Allie your mentor?"

She turns to me for a millisecond and pretends to barf. The she looks at Harry and says brightly. "Actually it wasn't a girl at all. It was Kirk Morrison."

FIFTY-ONE

I'm on my way to have my blood drawn, and seriously, I may throw up or pass out. The first time they took my blood was when I had a hundred-and-two fever for almost a week and was exhausted so everyone thought I had mono. I turned white right after, so they had to put cold compresses on my head until the blood came back to my face.

The second time they took blood was before I had my tonsils out and I threw up all over the waiting room of the lab. It's not that having blood drawn hurts that much. It's just a sickening thing to see that maroon-colored liquid oozing out of your arm and filling those glass tubes and knowing it's being sucked out of your veins like your life is being drained away.

But now, instead of dwelling on losing consciousness, I'm obsessed with replaying Amber's speech. I can't believe someone who keeps her thoughts under lock and key had the nerve to stand up and say what was on her mind. And also because what she said blew my mind.

Amber Augusta Bennington, the girl I always envied, the icon of beauty and perfection, stood up and told the whole class she envied me? That was a mind-blower. Unlike David, Amber didn't take my picture. But what she did give me was her picture of me—in words, as hard to believe as it is for me.

So, crazy as it is, I go into the lab with a new feeling in my gut. I see myself from a different perspective. The word "empowered" crosses my radar screen, the brainy equivalent of hotness. Other people want to be like me? Even envy me? Before today, thoughts like that never entered my mind. While music blasts on my iPhone, I stretch out my arm and focus on being in another sphere.

You can do this, Allie.

The needle stings, but I deal. A few minutes later, I walk outside into the cool air of a blindingly sunny day. I think of Mel and Katrina. They both went through this. Now I'm one step closer. Next week is my appointment with the medical photographer. Those pictures will be one set I definitely won't want to see.

✄----------

David and I are supposed to get coffee after school, but we don't. It's one of those days when the sun is out, the temperature is mild, and it feels like the entire earth is in bloom. So many people are on the streets that it looks like the whole world canceled work.

"Let's hang at the park," David says.

For the next two hours, we revisit our childhood. We sit on the cool metal swings and see who can swing the highest. We wait in line with two-year-olds to have a turn going down the slide. We sit on the seesaw and each of us tries to bump the other one up into the air like a missile, and then we run to the parallel bars and use our hands to cross them, even though I can't get to the end and David can.

"I'll walk you home," he says as we head for the path through the park. By the time we reach my block we're starved, so we stop for pizza.

"Is it okay if I order pepperoni?"

He cocks his head to the side. "Why wouldn't it be?"

"I thought the pepperoni might adulterate it." I'm deadpan. "Maybe it isn't the way purists order pizza."

"It's totally different from coffee with all the *additives*," he says. The word comes out as if he meant cyanide. "Pepperoni is definitely allowed."

It's four thirty in the afternoon and we're at Ray's Pizza. We're swiveling left and right on squeaky stools like we're dancing in place to the music. We're facing a wall of mirrors, and we're watching the pizza maker using his clenched fist like a pottery wheel to miraculously spin out a pizza crust from a mound of dough.

David is not wearing eye makeup today. His long eyelashes are a curious mix of brown and blond like some of them got sun bleached, and some didn't. He has amazing eyes. They're brown flecked with green, and I swear they change color with his moods, getting deeper when he's serious or angry, and almost electric green when he's laughing or fooling around.

There's a tiny yellow dot of pizza oil on the side of his lip that I'm tempted to wipe away as an excuse to touch him. He's drinking Coke from a can and staring at me over the rim. The light beams he's sending out are going through my pounding heart, every one a bull's-eye, sending tiny shock waves through me. The corners of my mouth turn up.

Yes, I have a definite crush on him.

He smiles and nods ever so slightly while he drinks.

He knows.

I don't have to say things for him to figure them out. We seem to communicate chemically on some deep, instinctual level.

Stealthily, he slides his camera out of his pocket and snaps my picture. Just one. No long continuous string of clicks. He looks down at it with a half smile on his face and holds the camera out to me.

I look at it and sit up straighter on the stool. "Not bad."

"Wrong," he says, shaking his head. "Beautiful."

FIFTY-TWO

It's not one of those dreams that take place sequentially. It's not logical like the soft-focused one about my surgery, where I'm in the operating room. This one has no beginning, middle, or end. I wake up and remember I was dreaming, but when I think back, it's more of a jumble, as if thoughts and feeling and images were bombarding my brain and I couldn't process everything coming at me fast enough to make order and sense out of it.

I'm sure some of it has to do with looking at the family picture album because I see pictures, lots of them, in a deep field that crosses time—my mom, my relatives, myself, even people I don't know—and they're all raining down on me. Some are David's pictures. Those are always on my mind because they're all of me.

The one he took in the pizza parlor after we went to the park stands out in particular. I'm smiling at him. It's kind of dreamy. Maybe that's why he likes it so much. As soon as he got home, he emailed it to me. I didn't have to ask if he printed it out. It's actually the best picture anyone has ever taken of me. I didn't tell him that, though. I was embarrassed to.

Something else I didn't tell him about is the surgery.

Just one week away.

And not his business. I don't need him to weigh in. It's not his face; it's mine. So why do I feel guilty? I ask Katrina what she thinks.

"Hmmm, that's a hard one. How would you feel if he didn't tell you something important?"

I don't have to think too long. "Betrayed?"

"I guess that's your answer."

The next day after school when we're walking out of the building and no one's nearby to hear, I turn to David. "I'm going to look different in a week."

He shakes his head, not understanding. "What?"

"I'm having my nose done."

He narrows his eyes and looks at me curiously. Then nothing. No comment. No grunts, no anything. He's thinking about it, though. I can tell from the way he's looking off. He shakes his head slightly.

"You wanna get something to eat?"

I'm not the least bit hungry. "Sure."

We take the subway to a Greek coffee shop in the Village and order stuffed grape leaves and hummus. We're sitting opposite each other in a banquette with fake leather seats and a table that's supposed to look like wood. While we wait for our order, I busy my hands and head by examining the sugar on the table, then the pepper and salt, wondering why someone decided that the tiny holes in the metal covers had to be in the shape of P and S when the bottles were clear and there was no way you could confuse them.

Then again, a lot of things don't make much sense, like the way two friends are suddenly acting like two strangers, sitting next to each other but barely talking. I stare at the posters on the walls, especially one of Santorini, a Greek island with houses that look like they're carved out of blocks of white chalk and crowned with sea-blue roofs that match the water and the sky. I imagine being there with David. We'd walk everywhere taking pictures. He looks at the poster too. If he's thinking the same thing, he doesn't let on.

A waiter with a thick head of curly gray hair and dark shining eyes that look like they know everything about the people he's serving puts our food on the table and smiles. I look at his eyes and glance away, embarrassed. As soon as he turns, we tear at the pita bread and finish everything except the olive pits.

David's quiet, staring off, his eyes taking in everyone in the restaurant except me. It bothers me. We talk briefly about speech, about Amber's talk.

"I bet she's not used to reaching into herself," he says. "She probably surprised herself when she wrote a decent speech." Something about that relates to me, his eyes seem to say.

Randomly I start talking about a new movie that we both want to see and an upcoming concert downtown. Then I run out of things to say. More dead silence. A wall is up and I don't know how to break it down. After we pay the bill and walk out to the street, he takes out his camera and snaps my picture.

"To remember you," David says. "The beautiful Allie. The real one."

I look at him and shake my head. *It's not your face; it's mine.* I didn't expect him to understand.

FIFTY-THREE

We slip our MetroCards through the gate and stand on the platform waiting for the Uptown subway. There's a newsstand, and I pretend to be interested in what's on the cover of *People*, *Newsweek*, and the *Daily News*. David's watching a rat that's walking along the subway tracks. It's hard to talk with the roar of the trains pulling into the station, but that's not why he's quiet. He looks wounded.

I'm annoyed at first. Whose body is it, whose life? Who is he to have an attitude? But then I think it means something if he's upset with the idea of me having surgery. Not that that changes anything. If he likes me now, he'll like me more after. And if he doesn't like me after, especially when I like me more after, then there probably wasn't much to the relationship anyway.

The moment we enter the train, he slumps down in his seat and stares at his camera, playing with it as if he's trying to figure out how to do some complex operation, even though I'm sure he knows every part of it as if he invented it himself. Just as a joke, I stick my face down under his and stare at him, but he avoids me, keeping his eyes on the camera, pretending not to see me.

I get up and move to a seat opposite him between two tough guys who look like professional wrestlers. They look like they wear size sixteen sneakers, and they're decked out with necklaces thick as bike chains. One of them, with bleached blond hair, is holding a paper bag with KFC inside that scents the air with eau de fried chicken. He's drinking soda from a sixty-four-ounce cup.

I fill the space between them. David looks up, momentarily concerned, but then he's back to camera scrutiny. I study the way his dark hair falls on the sides of his face, curling toward the angle of his chin, his intense eyes shadowed with some of the sooty eyeliner he wore the day before.

I take a magazine out of my bag, but instead of reading it, I cover one side of my face and peer at him with my left eye, unconcerned about the curious looks of people opposite me. Can I at least make him smile?

David sees me in his peripheral vision because suddenly, *click*, he takes a picture.

Yes, he's alive.

I cover the other eye. *Click*, another picture. I lower the magazine just below my eyes, covering my nose and mouth. He looks at me as if he's trying to memorize my face. I smile and look at him imploringly. *Smile back, please.* I want to get him out of his funky mind-set about the surgery. On the tip of my tongue is the expression, "It's not brain surgery."

But maybe that's exactly what it is—brain altering.

His eyes meet mine and hold them until we get to my stop. He jumps up and reaches for my hand, leading me out of the car and up the staircase out of the station. He's now bounding up the steps as though he was hit by a bolt of energy. As a joke, I start doing the "Amber Augusta Bennington I'm in love with myself" walk. Only now it feels right.

Without letting go of my hand, David walks me to my building. The dark cloud has magically lifted and we're back together, a couple.

Has he come to terms with the surgery?

My head is lighter now. Something in our relationship has changed. I feel as though David accepts what's going to happen. He's okay with it. He's okay with me. How did that happen? One thing I know for sure. He always seems to be one step ahead of his so-called mentor.

FIFTY-FOUR

When you have plastic surgery, you pay in advance. My
dad wrote a check to the doctor and we sent it in two weeks
ago. There's nothing left to do now except wait and worry. The
medical photographs were taken, the lab tests done. I passed
with flying colors. Now the sister sorority with Mel and Katrina
has gone from three to two to one.

I think back to our lunch at Saks and it seems like ages ago.
Mel told us about her consultation, and then she put her hand
into the middle of the table. Katrina's hand was over Mel's and
mine was on top.

"Strength in numbers," Mel said solemnly.

Only it doesn't feel that way anymore. Maybe in spirit they're
with me, but they've had the surgery and they've moved on. I'm
facing it alone. I call Mel more than she calls me. And Katrina
seems to be moving forward more than looking back to the

before life that I was a part of and remind her of. They don't check into the plastic surgery website anymore. Why should they? But I do. Am I looking for new friends there, replacements for them? I don't actually know why.

I find a website I haven't been to before. There's a bulletin board with posts about people's feelings before and after. A girl who is thinking of having her nose done says for her the surgery isn't really about how she looks, it's about how she feels. She says her surgeon told her, "If you're expecting a nose job to change your life, don't do it.

I think about how David and I have come together over the past few months, and how he celebrates how I look and how it's helped me feel more secure about myself. I'm not as compelled to look so hard in the mirror for answers.

But it's not just the attention from David. It's how he makes me feel. I'm not just a face with a nose. I'm someone who someone else likes, someone who's worthy. I'm a whole person who someone wants to be with after school and on weekends, because of who I am. It's not about my looks; it's about my soul.

Then there's the picture of my mom at the beach. The glow about her that has nothing to do with her appearance. It's about what's inside, how she feels about herself. I think about my DNA, that mysterious interior road map of my uniqueness and how it will remain the same even when the face I face the world with will change forever.

Will I be defying who I am?

Questions are swirling in my head, the tension binding me tightly as if I'm being held inside a straitjacket. I don't know where to turn. A phrase my mom uses over and over pops into my head.

Go with your gut.

Gut. Gut. My parents always say if your instincts tell you to do something, follow them. It's your body's way to keep you safe.

I pick up the phone.

The slow, deliberate thinking me is now powerless to stop the part of my brain in charge of survival that's been thrown into gear. I dial the number by heart. The secretary answers, but I don't want to talk to her. I know Dr. Miller's not in surgery today; it's his day to see patients in his office. I'm put on hold and every second makes the pounding in my head so loud I don't think I'll be able to hear.

I wait and wait. Whoever had the idea that piping music into the phone when you're on hold would make it more tolerable? It's some loud piece with drums and cymbals, obviously written by some tortured composer. Then suddenly the music dies. He picks up.

"Hello, Allie," he says. "How can I help you?" He's warm, compassionate. I need to hear that voice now.

"Dr. Miller," my voice says, in a rush.

"Yes?"

There's silence.

"Allie?"

"Dr. Miller…please…I want to cancel the surgery…I just need more time."

FIFTY-FIVE

I put down the phone with my shaking hand and sit back at my desk. I don't open Facebook. Or check email. I just stare at the screen saver, a photograph of a snow-covered field that seems to go on into infinity. It's quiet in the apartment. My mom and dad are still at work. The street outside is strangely calm. No honking horns. No sirens, just the steady white noise of traffic as my speeding heartbeat returns to normal like I'm in the walk phase after running a grueling race.

I look down at the rolling ring on my pinkie that Mel gave us and think about her and Katrina. What the three of us had seems a lifetime ago. They wouldn't get this, but that's okay. It's not about them. This is my nose. My face. And most of all, my life.

It's not about David either, but it's what he helped me see. Who I am isn't simple. I'm more than the face in the mirror or the image captured in a photograph. Those are like the opening sentences in a book, vital to get you drawn in, but not the whole story. That takes more time to develop. Life has chapters. It's complicated. And so are people.

I don't understand me yet. I'm a different me at different times, in different places. Life throws us curveballs just when we think we're on top of our game and understand everything about what we want.

It's not that I like my nose any more now or think everything's perfect. It's just that I want to try dwelling less on perfection and work at Google Mapping the way to finding out who I am.

After school the next day, David and I go for pizza, the everything kind with pepperoni, eggplant, roasted peppers, mushrooms, anchovies, and artichokes. David calls it "the works." He asks Mario, the pizza guy, for "the works." Mario knows him and laughs like it's some kind of inside joke between them.

"The works," Mario parrots back to David, before David snaps his picture. "The works, coming up."

David doesn't ask about the surgery and I don't talk about it. I see him studying me as I reach toward the counter to get my soda, and I turn to him.

"How did you know?"

He knows. He doesn't have to ask what I'm talking about.

"You're the kind of girl who likes 'the works,'" he says. "No pizza lite."

I raise an eyebrow. "What?"

"Remember mentoring? And grammar?"

"So?"

"I told you I wasn't going to write books, so why did I have to learn it."

I wait.

"It's important, you said, because these are the rules that you should know, whether you choose to follow them or not."

I still must look confused.

"Allie," he says like I'm a dimwit. "You want the most out of life. You're not happy with just writing a sentence. You have to know how to diagram it. You need to know about the right words. And their derivation. I mean, c'mon. Most people in the world don't care, but you do. You're different."

"But the surgery? How did you know I wouldn't do it?"

"There was one picture I took of you. The one I called beautiful. You liked it too."

I can't help smiling.

"The camera showed you something new…"

"What?"

"Confidence," he says. "You were there. There was this light in your eyes. You owned your face."

"And cameras never lie."

"That's right," he says softly. And then he kisses me.